The Dragon Amulet

Family Relics Book 3

by

Tanya Miranda

The Dragon Amulet
By Tanya Miranda

Cover by Seedlings Design Studio
www.seedlingsonline.com

Published by Blue Dragonfly Publishing
www.bluedragonflypublishing.com

ISBN-13: 978-1-7323919-1-8
ISBN-10: 1-7323919-1-2

For my brother, Norberto,
you would have loved the ending.

THE UNFORESEEABLE

(SEVENTY YEARS AGO)

Standing at the foot of the ocean, Agatha clasps the metal charm hanging around her neck, closes her eyes, and waits for a sign. The sunset rays warm her cheeks. She recalls the faces of beloved coven sisters who have been dead for centuries and landscapes of childhood places that no longer exist. She whispers an ancient prayer, begging the spirits of her ancestors for forgiveness, pleading for Mother Nature's approval of her decision.

Pacific Ocean waves brush against her ankles, wetting the folded edges of her slacks as she replays her life's most pivotal moments. Happier memories flicker, vague and grainy, but images of death present themselves with perfect clarity. As the waves retreat, a resounding guilt weighs her down, as if pressing her feet deeper into the wet sand. She squeezes her hand tightly around the charm.

A tear streams down her cheek as she remembers the promise she made to her mother, Finna, before she died.

A yellow beam of moonlight stretched from the window to where her mother lay in her bed. Finna coughed, and Agatha rushed to offer her a handkerchief. Once the cough settled down, Agatha knelt and gently brushed white strands of hair away from her mother's face. Then she handed Finna her knife.

With the little strength she had left, Finna cut her palm to produce blood for the handshake that would seal their deal. Agatha sliced her own palm, took Finna's hand in her own, and shook it

1

with determination.

"A blood promise is never broken," Finna said from her deathbed. Struggling against the intoxicating pull of surrender, Finna tugged on Agatha's arm and whispered between heavy breaths, "Swear to me you will never . . . use the spell . . . unless your life is at stake. Do not . . . take it for granted. Swear to it."

Agatha nodded. "I swear, Mother. I will never use it unless my life is at stake."

The promise echoes in her ears as a gust of ocean wind whips her auburn hair away from her face. She gazes at the majestic silhouette of the recently built Golden Gate Bridge, following its metallic lines to the mountains across the bay.

Man is capable of such magnificent creations, and such horrific destruction.

As Agatha's mind is bombarded by memories of war, two seagulls cut across the sky, breaking her reverie. They dive toward the sand, exposing their claws and flapping their wings wildly in a fight for a small loaf of bread. The dominant seagull pecks the other in the chest and kicks at his wings, forcing it away. Three more seagulls swoop down, and a rumble ensues. Their beaks collide, wings flapping violently, and loud squawks echo across the beach. They flip pieces of bread in the air as they shred the loaf into inedible pieces. More seagulls join the fight, shoving the smaller, weaker birds. Some get a piece of the loaf before it's destroyed, and several seagulls are left wanting.

Vicious little things. There was enough bread for all of them.

The squabble reminds her of the conflict between her mother's coven and the Foreman Clan. Finna had married Agatha's father, Caderyn, the leader of the Foreman Clan, to form a union and keep the peace between the rival groups. It was the first union of its kind—both Finna and Caderyn were leaders of a

2

community of sorcery, possessing distinct powers and abilities.

Although both nations had supporters and detractors, no one doubted the union as aggressively as the other Foreman Clan leaders. They claimed Finna was untruthful to her husband and accused her of bewitching Caderyn—a crime punishable by death. Finna had no choice but to take young Agatha and flee the clan in the pitch darkness of the night.

Finna's betrayal fueled a lust for revenge within the Foreman Clan's leadership, and eventually in Caderyn himself.

The seagull fight rolls toward Agatha, and she stands and shouts at the scuffle, scaring the birds into flight. She buries what's left of the bread under the sand and returns to her blanket on the beach, enjoying the silence. Peace is all she wants—it's all she and her mother ever wanted—but sometimes, wanting peace isn't enough. Sometimes, you must prepare for the worst.

And Finna did just that.

In preparation for retaliation by the Foreman Clan, Finna gave life to the Gregorn Dragons. Agatha grew up alongside those young dragons, playing with them and learning how to control them—and how to fight with them against common enemies. Agatha learned everything she could from Finna and the other sisters in her coven, and eventually grew up to be a powerful sorceress herself.

It took years, as wars did in those times, but once war arrived, the dragons proved their worth. Caderyn and the Foreman Clan army were defeated, diminished into a fraction of their former glory, and a new era of peace and hope arrived for Finna's coven . . . or so they thought.

Agatha shakes her head. *How naive I was back then, to think that the destruction of the Foreman Clan meant peace for us.*

Soon after Finna passed away, the dragons rebelled against the coven. Whatever betrayals she recalls between her parents, between the two nations, it was nothing compared to the way the Gregorn Dragons betrayed Agatha.

Acid fills her mouth, and she spits to the side.

Memories wash over her relentlessly, overtaking her mind like a small child knocked over by a crashing wave. The charred remains of her sisters, their homes and villages reduced to ashes, her island home transformed into a land of fire and soot.

Agatha wipes the tears from her cheeks.

No one in the coven anticipated the dragon rebellion—especially not Agatha. She had inherited Finna's maternal bond with the dragons, grown up with them, received battle scars alongside them, considered them as part of her family. When they rebelled and nearly annihilated the coven, they broke her heart. She has been living with this broken heart ever since.

For centuries.

The aged black leather rope breaks easily when Agatha yanks the pendant off her neck, as if the rope was ready to be broken. Holding it up against the sunset, she squints at the charm's oval shape, and then lowers it to remove the rope from the loop. A dull shine gleams off the dragon etched into the amulet before she flips it over to reveal the engraving on the back.

"Death cannot be avoided, even by magic," she whispers.

A thick knot forms in her throat.

Agatha lifts her eyes toward the sunset and closes her fist once more. She presses her fist against her chest and sends one final message out into the universe before setting out to fulfill her goal.

My dearest mother—you sacrificed everything you knew to save the coven. You weren't sure the spell would work. You feared you would die if you executed it incorrectly. But if you didn't try, death was imminent. And you succeeded. You turned back time and changed everything. You saved the coven.

Agatha swallows hard. She is thankful her mother died of old age and never experienced the dragons' betrayal.

I know the price of the time-reversal spell was hefty. You never met your husband, and you never had the children you loved dearly. They never existed in your new lifetime, and I know how much you've suffered. I have not forgotten a single detail of your sacrifice. I know it all by heart. Your memories are my memories. Your pain is my pain.

She closes her eyes tight, takes another deep breath, and grimaces.

But I am not you. I do not have a family to lose. I have not been able to live a normal life or find any semblance of happiness. I continue to live with the images of my dead sisters in my nightmares, and in my thoughts. I have no light to shine them away into the shadows, no love of any kind to heal my pain. I am living day by day in misery and loneliness. Our coven may have survived war with the Foreman Clan, but we barely survived the Gregorn Dragons' rebellion. Centuries later, I still can't get over it.

Agatha opens her eyes to allow more tears to flow and gazes upon the setting sun behind the clouds as if it is listening to her pleas.

Worse, I possess the power to undo the dragon rebellion, to go back to that time and fix what has been broken. My inability to find the Isle of Enid kept me from executing it. But now, after spending the last few decades in desperate search of it, I have finally found a way. I can feel the certainty of this in my bones. Now, my only obstacle is the promise I made to you.

Agatha inhales a shaky breath and swallows hard at the memory of her mother lying on her deathbed. Their blood intermingling in the handshake, the fearful yet hopeful look in her mother's eyes.

I don't have an immediate threat as you did when you

executed the spell. My life is not in danger. But . . . I can't go on living this way when I have the chance to change it. I have a chance to change history and make a better life . . . for me and the coven.

Squeezing the relic tighter, Agatha lowers her head.

I'm not as strong as you were, Mother. I was never as strong as you. I'm sorry, but I have to break my promise. Please forgive me.

Decades ago, when Agatha begged the mountains and trees for guidance in locating the Isle of Enid, nature fell silent. She hasn't felt a connection with the natural world since. It was as if she faced punishment for trying to break her promise. Nature abandoned her and left her to wander alone.

But now, a cool ocean breeze caresses Agatha's cheeks, urging her to lift her chin. She takes a deep breath and accepts nature's love, nature's wind-guided embrace, a feeling she hasn't had in a long time. She interprets nature's response as its acceptance of her apology, its forgiveness of her weakness, its approval of her decision, and she releases a soft cry.

The time-reversal spell is the panacea for all her suffering, and now she can go after it without guilt.

Agatha stands and takes the first steps of her long-awaited journey, but a large golden retriever puppy runs at her from behind at full speed, knocks her to her knees, and smothers her with wet licks and nose nuzzles. The attack lasts for a few seconds, then someone pulls the baby beast away and helps her to her feet.

When Agatha gazes upon her savior's ocean-blue eyes and wide, honest smile, she takes a long breath and smiles back.

And just like that, as nature or the powers that be intended, Elliot McKeery, a young man strolling carefree along a California beach with his oversized, rambunctious golden retriever puppy, thwarts Agatha's plans and steals her heart.

PROMISES

The lounge chair in Brian's hospital room isn't as comfortable as Jasmyn had hoped. When she wakes up, she reaches lazily for her cell phone buzzing on the windowsill and silences the alarm. After stretching her arms and straightening her back, while groaning at the stiffness in her neck, she stands and draws the thin plastic blinds, allowing the morning sky to brighten the dreary room.

"Good morning," Brian whispers as he wakes up, his sleepy smile full of optimism. "You're up early."

Jasmyn steps toward the bed. "Did you sleep well?"

"As good as any other 'scientific wonder.'" He shifts over to give Jasmyn room to sit next to him on the bed. "What time is it?"

"Seven thirty."

He wrinkles his nose. "Why are you up so early?"

"Thought I'd get a few minutes with you before the probing started."

"If only you could tell them Regina healed me, then they'd stop trying to figure out how my brain injuries 'miraculously' disappeared."

"Yeah, but then they'd stick us all in the psych ward."

He groans. "How different would that be? I'm already under observation."

She rubs her neck. "The more they think we had nothing to do with your recovery, the better. We're already under surveillance after all the destruction at the airport last week with the Foreman Clan, and the week before with the Gregorn Dragons. If the doctors find out Regina has healing powers, they'll take us all in for observation."

"I guess I can take one for the team, as long as the probing doesn't get *too* invasive."

Jasmyn tilts her head. "What do you think they're going to do?"

He shrugs, a twinkle in his eyes. "As long as they don't stick things where things don't belong . . ."

"I'm sure it won't come to that." She smirks.

He gazes at her face and blinks slowly. "How are you feeling? Are you back to normal?"

"Well, I'm not a 'medical marvel' like you, but I'm good. I was able to perform some elemental spells yesterday without collapsing from exhaustion, finally."

"What I mean is . . ." Brian places his left hand over his heart. "How are you feeling here?"

Jasmyn lowers her eyes. The daylight draws her attention, and she stands and walks to the window. "I'm better, I guess. If I keep busy, I try not to remember . . . or think about . . ."

How different might her life be if she hadn't been so jealous and resentful of her little sister?

If only she'd loved Katarina more, forgiven her for offenses that seem so trivial now, then maybe Jasmyn wouldn't have broken the enchanted box that housed the Gregorn Dragons and started the chain of events that led to Katarina's and Logan's deaths.

She gazes out the window and drifts off in a sea of endless doubts.

"Jaz?"

A plane in the sky draws her attention, and she inhales

quietly when Brian touches her hand. She smiles at him softly. "I'm fine."

"Are you sure? You know you can talk to me, right?"

Although everyone has told her repeatedly that her siblings' deaths aren't her fault, she still blames herself. Her self-blame is driving her to the Isle of Enid to execute the time-reversal spell and undo everything. This guilt fuels her forward. She can't shake it.

She won't.

Jasmyn owns it, and she's become an expert at lying about it.

She waves her right hand and rolls her eyes aloofly. "I'm alright, really. I'm better than before. I'm just exhausted. Patricia had me executing elemental spells all week. I think I hit my limit yesterday. It was a long day. The drive from Upstate New York was also tiring."

He furrows his brows. "Are you getting stronger?"

"A lot stronger, actually. I was finally able to move mountains without collapsing."

"Are you expecting another Foreman Clan battle?"

"No, but Patricia says it's always better to be ready for anything."

A young hospital orderly taps on the door and walks in with a tray of food. "Breakfast time," she says with a wide grin.

"Yes, please! Put it by the window." Brian rises slowly from his bed, grunting as he stands and shuffles to the bathroom.

When Brian returns, he sits at the small table, picks up a piece of buttered toast from his tray, and stuffs it in his mouth. He pushes the small bagel to the side. "The bagels here suck. I'd do anything for a fresh onion bagel with cream cheese."

Jasmyn sits across from him. "You can't expect too much from hospital food."

He scarfs down the scrambled eggs, toast, and ham in less than a minute and shovels the strawberry yogurt into his mouth with two large scoops. The orange juice bottle seems to drain instantly. He finishes his breakfast with a sigh of satisfaction and prepares his coffee with milk and sugar.

Jasmyn simply watches with a big smile on her face. "Hungry much?"

"It's like I can't be satisfied. Last night, I had steak and potatoes and greens and bread and . . . and I was still hungry." He takes a sip of his coffee.

"Regina said you'd have a huge appetite once you're healed. The magic blends your own energy with hers to heal you."

With a shrug, he said, "All I know is that I'm always hungry."

Jasmyn reaches for the small bowl of grapes.

He playfully slaps her hand. "Hey, those are my grapes! I'm in recovery here." He stabs a piece of melon with his fork and hands it to her. "Take the melon slices. I hate melon."

"I hate melons too." She smiles and sits back in her chair. "Don't worry. I'll just get a fresh onion bagel on the way to the airport."

"That's not nice."

"Toasted, with cream cheese. Maybe two. One for breakfast and another for the flight."

He smirks and pushes the bowl of grapes toward her.

After picking a few grapes, she pushes the bowl back to his side of the table.

"I wish I could go with you to Manchester," he said. "I've never been to England."

"Me neither. But we're not on vacation—we're there to get the details of the time-reversal spell from Ryland, and then we're heading to the Isle of Enid. Doubt I'll see anything

10

interesting."

"Are you kidding? Dingy dungeons, creepy alleyways, cobblestone streets. There are like hundreds of castles and churches. There's probably a four-hundred-year-old church in the airport. Ryland probably lives in one of them."

"Actually, I think he does."

Brian gasps. "I'm so jealous right now."

She plops a grape into her mouth and smirks. "We have old churches and cobblestone streets here too."

"Yeah, but they weren't built three centuries ago. Our country isn't even that old. I mean, what—if anything—have you seen, in the United States, that's more than three hundred years old?"

Without skipping a beat, Jasmyn says, "Patricia."

Brian chortles and swallows his grapes. "She doesn't look a day over two hundred."

"She's a young sorceress, like Regina."

"Right, young, like Regina. Seriously, though." Brian clears his throat. "Maybe I can meet up with you in Manchester in a few days. The doctor said I should be back to normal as long as I eat well, rest, and do my therapy for the muscle atrophy." He finishes his coffee in one last gulp. "The neurosurgeon scheduled an intense session today." He flexes his right arm. "I'll be tip-top."

"Tip-top?" Jasmyn raises an eyebrow.

"Yep. Fit as a fiddle. The bee's knees. The dog's bollocks."

She giggles. "What does any of that mean?"

"I've been researching British slang." He laughs and pops the last of the grapes into his mouth. "Just let me know where you're staying, and I'll fly over once I get the okay from the doctor."

"I don't know where we'll be in a few days. Manchester is the starting point. There's no set itinerary. Patricia's planning as we go."

A crinkle forms in Brian's eyebrows. He sits back in his chair. "Okay. So . . . when will you be back?"

Her stomach tightens, and she clears her throat. "We have to find Ryland and the Isle of Enid, and . . . we may be gone for a few days or weeks. And if we learn how to execute the spell . . ."

A frown appears on Brian's face, and he gazes at the cream colored hospital floor. Although nothing has changed in their plans, Jasmyn knows he can sense her hesitation, her uncertainty. He doesn't ask any more questions and stands to face the window.

Brian's emotions crash against her aura, both caressing and jabbing her skin ever so slightly—love, anxiety, fear, hope—contradicting sensations battling for attention. The ability to physically sense a person's intentions, their truest emotions, is a skill Jasmyn knows well.

And even though Brian can't verbally tell her everything he's feeling, one thing Jasmyn knows with certainty from reading his aura is that he truly loves her.

A knot forms in her throat, and she opens her mouth to say she's eager to return to him, to be with him, but nothing comes out. Returning would mean the failure of her mission, and that is something she can't allow.

She must travel back to a time before she reunited with Brian, before any of this ever happened, before they fell in love. She knows Brian won't love her the way he loves her now. They won't go through the intense trials and losses that have brought them close to one another as they did in this life. In her new life, Jasmyn will get Katarina and Logan back, but she will lose Brian's love.

Success will be bittersweet, but failure is unthinkable. If she doesn't find a way to go back, she can never return to Brian.

Jasmyn will never allow herself to be happy. Katarina and Logan are dead because of her. Her parents have lost two children because of her. Leaving Brian is her penance for all the misery she has caused.

No matter what happens, these are their last moments together.

Two nurses walk into the hospital room with clipboards, and Jasmyn stands up and grabs her jacket.

"Wait," Brian says to the nurses. "My girlfriend is leaving for a few weeks. Can you give us a few moments to say goodbye?"

One of the nurses smiles at them and nudges the other nurse with her elbow. "Of course. We'll be right outside."

Once the door closes, Brian takes hold of both her hands. "Remember what I said, if . . . *when* you go back in time, come find me."

Jasmyn's eyes tear up. "You know it won't be the same."

"Remember the letters I wrote to you and never sent? They're in the green shoebox in the back of my closet. I never told anyone about them. If you tell me about those letters, I'll know you're telling me the truth."

"You'll think I broke into your apartment and went through your things."

"I won't. The letters are in a sealed plastic zip bag. It's taped up. It will still be taped."

"Brian, you'll think I'm crazy."

"I won't." He looks deep into her eyes. "Just promise me you'll look for me and tell me everything. I just know I'll believe you."

"But . . . Brian . . . I—"

"Promise me!" he says in a stern voice, squeezing her hands.

Jasmyn nods, knowing full well she doesn't mean it.

After a breath, he grabs her at the waist and pulls her in for a deep kiss. He holds her there for several seconds, pressing her body as close as he possibly can, and then releases her.

"Promise me," he whispers, breathless.

"I . . ."

He kisses her once more, deeper than before. A tear flows down his cheeks and rolls onto her lips. When he pulls away, he whispers weakly, his bottom lip trembling. "Swear to it."

"I swear," Jasmyn says. "I swear, I will find you."

2

ENCHANTED SEAS

Joseph Tiller steps to the edge of his fishing boat and imagines the steaks he'll eat tonight once his assignment is complete. Icy sea winds graze his nose as his boat drifts off the northern coast of Iceland. He faces north toward Greenland, past the looming gray clouds, and pulls out a paper with the instructions Ryland sent earlier. Although it's an odd assignment, a gig is a gig, and the payout is too good to resist.

He walks out to the deck and finds his crewmen waiting.

"He's going to read a poem," Shawn, the first mate, says flatly.

"Read a poem? To who?" Clark positions himself next to Shawn and buttons up his peacoat. He combs his fingers through his black locks and stuffs his hair neatly under his fisherman's hat.

"No one, really. He has to read it out toward the sea."

Jack, the oldest of the crew by a few decades, grunts and then spits over the rail. "It's a curse. He'll damn us all, I tell you. He'll awaken Rán, and then we'll have hell to pay."

Sid, the youngest, with only two seafaring years under his belt, arrives at the rail last and stands next to Clark. He leans over and looks at Shawn with innocent eyes. "Is that true?"

"Don't be daft, Sid. It's just Jack and his old-man superstitions. It's just a poem, probably from a lovesick fool."

Sid swallows hard. "Who's Rán?"

"Goddess of the sea." Jack huffs, scratches his wiry beard, and then grunts again. "But don't let that fool you—she's the stuff

15

of nightmares. You don't want to be on the bad side of her."

Shawn rolls his eyes and shakes his head. He leans toward Sid. "Don't listen to him. He's so full of stories he can't tell the real ones from the fake ones anymore."

"Aye, I may be old, but I know not to tempt the gods of the sea, especially when you're on them."

"Relax." Joseph walks to the edge of the ship and looks back at the four crewmen. "It's just a poem. I don't want to hear any more talk about sea gods, myths, or curses. This is the twenty-first century; we're a lot smarter than that."

Jack huffs again and mumbles, "Even brilliant men are swallowed up by the sea."

Joseph shoots him a glare. "That's enough, Jack." The boat bounces on a choppy wave, and Joseph bends his knees to keep his balance. "This one job will pay us more than we ever made ferrying across the ports, more than we've made in months." Joseph looks at each of the sailors. "Who wants to get paid?"

"Aye," they all respond, except for Jack.

"Who wants to eat like kings tonight?"

"Aye."

"Well, then, let's get on with it. Shawn, ready with the camera?"

"Aye, Captain."

Joseph takes off his black hat, finger-combs his hair, and straightens his peacoat as if trying to impress someone. He glances at the instructions once more and digs into his pocket to pull out the black gemstone Ryland included in the package.

"Ready, boys?" he asks with a smirk, then faces northward, as detailed in the letter.

Stretching the black gemstone toward the northern horizon, Joseph clears his throat and recites the poem, reading each line in a monotonous voice. He chortles halfway through and shakes his head, feeling silly in front of these men who have served him for years. After regaining his composure, he finishes the poem halfheartedly. A few seconds pass as he scans the deck and the ocean. He looks back at his crew, winks at the camera, and chuckles.

Clark and Sid sigh in relief. After another second, they're all laughing.

"See, Jack?" Shawn slaps the old man on the shoulder. "It's just a poem, an odd one at that—but still just a poem."

Jack grunts and spits over the rail.

"Alright, fellas. Let's do it once more. This time, no one make a sound. It has to be a clean recording. I don't want this guy to have any reason to say I didn't follow his instructions to the letter."

"Maybe you should say it louder, Captain," Clark says with a grin. "And with feeling. It is a poem, after all."

Joseph smirks. "Alright. Everyone quiet now. Ready, Shawn?"

"Camera's rolling."

"Here we go."

With the stone still in hand, Joseph recites the spell again, but this time he speaks in a slow, thundering voice, pausing between each line as the spell requires, and with his right hand stretched out to the sea, directing the poem to the edge of the world. He enunciates each phrase at the correct point, emphasizing specific words, with deep emotion, as if he wrote it himself.

Northern winds of northern seas,
I beg you for your help this night.
Northern winds of northern seas,
Please send this message 'round the world.
Northern winds of northern seas,

Send word to Finna's captive bird:
Rise, my darling, from your sleep,
For Ryland waits for your embrace.
Fly fast to seek your destiny.

After a few silent seconds, Shawn stops recording. "Got it. That was great, Cap. A clean recording. No giggles whatsoever."

Clark huffs. "That was uneventful."

"What were you expecting?" Shawn chuckles. "A daemon to jump out of the water, tentacles flailing?"

"Look at Sid," Clark says, laughing, "he's white as a ghost!"

The crewmen's laughter fade far away behind Joseph. Although Joseph remains standing on the deck, staring out to the edges of the ocean, his body feels weightless, as if he's floating above the water away from the boat toward the horizon. The black gemstone falls into the sea as his arm returns to his side. He hears the hypnotic melody of Loritida's sultry voice.

"Come to me, Joseph," she whispers in his mind. "I am Loritida, your mistress. Come to me."

In the distance, the breathtaking image of a beautiful woman reaches out to him. Her jet-black hair drapes over her shoulders as she curls her fingers. "Come to me, Joseph."

Joseph can't look away from her crystal-blue eyes. He doesn't want to. Loritida has him under her control now, and he doesn't fight it.

After calling out his name several times, Shawn yanks Joseph's arm, turning him around and breaking the trance. "Captain! Are you okay?"

"I'm . . ." Joseph looks at Shawn's worried face, then at the water. He raises his eyes toward the horizon and whispers, "I am your servant, Loritida, and I will come for you."

"What?" Shawn says.

Two quiet breaths later, a low rumble beneath the water slowly grows into an earthquake. The surface rises into a large wave, lifting the boat up to the sky in one fell swoop. The men brace themselves against the rails and scream in terror. When the ship reaches its highest altitude and seems to be floating in midair, the men stop screaming.

Everything goes quiet.

Several seconds pass as the crewmen glance at each other with fright, clasping their crosses and other holy relics, whispering prayers of deliverance.

A few seconds later, the wave slowly flattens out, and the ocean is tranquil once more.

Joseph, who stood strong and tall during the supernatural event, commands, "I've got our next destination. Prepare for departure."

The crewmen crouch on the floor of the deck, recovering from the ordeal, still praying. Joseph steps up to each man with a glare. Each sailor rises but averts his eyes upon seeing the deep blackness in Joseph's stare.

Once all four men stand at attention, with their eyes aimed at the deck and their legs shaking, Joseph turns around. "Prepare for departure."

"Aye, Captain," they all respond with trembling voices.

Without another word, Joseph heads to the control room.

3

READING THE SIGNS

A penetrating chill wakes Regina from a deep sleep, and she rises into a seated position on her hotel bed. The air-conditioned room is even colder now that she's covered in sweat, and she grabs the flower-print polyester quilt.

Trembling, she bends over to keep the nausea at bay.

Regina recalls her mother's advice on treating these nauseating sensations as warnings from nature. She closes her eyes and remembers her mother's words.

"Trust your instincts, Regina. You will know when nature is trying to tell you something."

With the quilt wrapped around her shoulders, Regina stands and walks to the window to push open the blackout curtains. The blue morning sky brightens the room and makes her squint. Her temples throb, her stomach gurgles, and she heads to the bathroom to throw up.

After emptying out her belly and washing her face, Regina picks up her phone on the nightstand and dials Patricia.

"I said only emergencies," Patricia says grumpily, half-asleep on the other side of the call. "This better be important."

"It is." Regina lifts her suitcase onto the bed. "I feel . . . something."

"Regina," Patricia shoots back. "It's eight thirty in the morning. I was up until three a.m. Can you be more specific? What's the emergency?"

"I don't know yet, I just . . . I'm feeling something deep."

Patricia releases a long sigh, and groans.

"It's like a strong energy, a pull, a heavy . . . I don't know how to explain it. Remember how I felt when Agatha died, when the Gregorn Dragons were released? It's similar. My body is shaking, I have cold sweats, and I feel sick to my stomach. Something big is happening."

"Great. Like we need another omen." Patricia moans, then sighs. "I wonder why nature never sends me any signals."

"Could it be because you're so defensive and dismissive?"

"Maybe."

Regina rolls her eyes and closes her suitcase. She puts on a jean jacket over her dress. "You just suck at it. I'm more open-minded. I let the universe in if it knocks on my door."

Laughter carries over the call. "The universe, Mother Nature, the hot young soldier escorting us to the airport."

"Patricia, I'm serious. There's no time to laugh."

"Oh, come on, Regina, there's always time to laugh. You're a light-hearted, open-minded spirit. What is life without a few giggles?"

"Fine, you can make jokes. I've got to get to a nature preserve."

"We're on Long Island. There isn't one for miles."

Regina places Patricia on speaker and sets the phone on her bed. "Maybe in New Jersey, along the Appalachian Trail." She tugs on her brown hiking boots and silently considers how her grimy boots don't match her floral dress, then shrugs. "There are a lot of untouched mountains in Jersey. I can go to the highest point and—"

"We're flying to Manchester this evening. The flight leaves at six. You have to be at the airport by four!"

"I know."

Regina sets her purse on the dresser and throws her

belongings into her bag. She grabs her sunglasses and her car keys jangle in her hands.

"Gustavo arranged this flight for us. You have to be there by six or—"

"I know! I won't be late."

"Regina!"

She picks up the phone and walks out of the hotel room with her suitcase in tow. "I have to do this. I can't let this pass. It's early—I'll drive out to New Jersey and be back before you know it."

"I swear, Regina, if you miss this flight—"

"I won't." She pulls the phone away from her face for a few seconds so Patricia won't hear her loud burp.

"We will leave without—"

Regina hangs up, rolls her eyes, and jogs to her car.

~ ~ ~

Just as Jasmyn is about to pay for her breakfast order at the delicatessen, a sharp pain strikes her gut and she stifles a cry. She bends over and moans, leaning against the deli counter.

"Are you alright?" the cashier asks.

Jasmyn nods. "Just a sec," she grunts out. After several deep breaths, the pain subsides, and she straightens and nods again. "I'm fine."

The sensation isn't completely gone, but it's bearable, so she takes the bag of bagels to her car. Once she slumps into the driver's seat, she breathes deeply and concentrates on the pain in her stomach.

What the hell is this? I only ate a few grapes.

Another burp.

I bet Regina has a quick stomachache-curing spell.

A truck cruising down the street draws her attention upward. After it passes, she spots a pharmacy across the street. She purses her lips.

"Antacids."

Upon her return from the pharmacy, chewing a few antacid tablets as the packaging suggests, she takes a sip from a water bottle, then grunts as her stomach gurgles. She sits back and waits.

"Come on antacids . . . do your thing!"

She waits a few more minutes and takes another a sip. Her stomach tightens, as if rejecting the treatment.

Maybe the grapes were bad, or maybe I caught a stomach flu at the hospital, or . . .

An idea enters her mind, and she gasps.

Could this be a message?

Her eyes dart wildly across the components of the dashboard.

Could nature be talking to me? I mean . . . Regina said warnings feel like bad headaches and stomachaches, the kind that knock you over. This one's bad. I've never had one so strong before . . . not that I can recall.

She presses her lips together.

I took antacids. I've burped repeatedly. This must be nature trying to communicate with me. Maybe it's a warning.

She pulls out her phone and searches for Regina's contact info.

It's a warning. I just know it!

4

EXILED

Weeks ago, on the day Agatha died, Loritida woke up gasping in an icy cave on a bed of dried-out hay. After hundreds of years of sleep, her body was weak from atrophy and covered in fungus and sores.

She blinked repeatedly, unable to move her arms or legs, and tried her best to open her mouth—but the rotten paste and moss made it difficult. Using her feeble arms and shoulders, Loritida dragged herself to the cave wall and pushed herself to a seated position. She scanned the darkness for a few minutes, trying to make sense of what had happened, of what had prompted her to wake.

Something is different.

As soon as Loritida felt it, she gasped.

Finna's blood spell that had trapped her on this island, the oppressive weight of her prison sentence, this centuries-long punishment, was suddenly gone.

Can it be? Has Finna finally released me from my prison? Am I truly free?

She smiled through the rot in her mouth and released a soft cry.

Oh, Finna, I have learned my lesson. No more dark magic. Ever again.

A growl roared in her stomach and echoed in the cave, and her entire body ached, from her head all the way down her spine to her toes. She could barely move, but when she heard the tiny patter of a bug skittering down the cave wall, her dry mouth began to water.

In the pitch-black darkness, with deadly precision, she slapped her hand on the bug and shoved the critter into her mouth. The crunch, however disgusting it might be to most people, was a sense of relief. She had a lot of work to do to get her strength back—this bug was only the beginning.

After a few days, her legs were still immobile. Moving around the cave was nearly impossible. She concentrated on strengthening her muscles with the little magic she had, but most days she slept long hours to help her recovery. The sleep spell she'd placed upon herself over a hundred years ago might have saved her from madness, but her body had deteriorated, and her magical abilities diminished.

She had to be in presentable shape when Finna arrived. She could not let the coven see her like this.

After a week, Loritida finally regained enough strength to drag her body around the cave with ease. Sitting up was becoming easier, as was catching larger vermin. Her legs were still weak, but she'd regained some sensation in her toes.

"What has it been, four hundred years since Finna sent me to this prison?" she asked the three wolf skulls on the rock next to her bed of hay. She set up her personal council long before she put herself to sleep to keep her sanity. They were covered in webs, dirt, and dust when she awoke, but she cleaned them off. Their polished bone glowed in the dark cave.

"Why hasn't she come? Do any of you have any ideas?"

The skulls did not answer.

"Do you think she's still angry with me? No? You're right. How could she be? I have suffered far more than she."

She gazed deep into each empty eye socket before drifting off into a memory of her daughter's death. She shook her head.

"What's done is done. Finna must have a plan. Although she would have contacted me by now. I wonder . . ."

An unsuspecting rat ran into the cave, seeking shelter from the northern storm.

"Finally," she whispered. "I've been waiting for you for days."

She held completely still as the tiny animal sniffed its way around the cave and eventually reached her toes. Then she snatched up the creature in one hand. It squealed just before she broke its neck.

"Why don't we find out what Finna's up to?" Loritida said to the three skulls with a bit of excitement.

She dragged herself several feet to a hole full of water that had dripped from icicles hanging overhead. She poked out the rat's eyes and tossed the bloody spheres into the icy pool, then broke the bracelet off her wrist and dipped it into her concoction. The rope bracelet was a gift from Finna when they were young girls threading jewelry.

Until this day, even after Finna had sentenced her to exile, Loritida had never taken it off. She knew these tokens would come in handy one day.

Upon the third attempt at the vision spell, an image appeared in the water. A young woman stood at the edge of a mountain, looking out toward the sunset, with the same auburn hair and deep-set eyes as Finna. The vision lasted for a few seconds before Loritida's arms gave out and she coughed and choked on her own spit. Her body still needed more healing for such exertion, and her arms could only hold her up for so long.

"So, Finna's dead." Loritida crawled back to her bed of hay. "I wonder how she died. Who is the leader of the coven?" She furrowed her eyebrows at her council. "And who was that girl? Any ideas?"

She imagined their response and jerked her head back. "You're right! She must be Finna's kin. Why else would she appear in my vision? But what's her name? Why did she release me? Tell me!"

The council went silent.

Loritida grunted with frustration and laid flat on her bed. As dozens of questions floated in her mind, her furrowed eyebrows relaxed, and her lips twisted into a snarl. "I hope Finna died a gruesome death."

After a few days of rest and recovery, Loritida attempted the vision spell again. This time, she held the visions in the water for several minutes longer. She saw Finna's kin crying about her little sister's death. A woman with long hair the color of midnight consoled her. Her face seemed familiar, but Loritida could not place her in her memories. Alongside the woman stood another with bright red locks curling down her shoulders, also crying.

Although Loritida didn't immediately identify the two women, their magical auras were undeniable. She narrowed her eyes toward the vision in the water, pressed her hands into tight fists, held her breath, and concentrated. She repeated the spell again as details of the vision became unraveled.

"Patricia . . . Regina . . . Jasmyn . . . Jasmyn is Finna's kin."

Her arms gave out. She coughed hard and spit up blood.

"Where arc the other sisters'? What happened to them?"

The images in the water disappeared.

"Why hasn't Jasmyn come for me?"

Loritida slowly lost consciousness on the cave floor.

A few more days passed, and Loritida's cough was not as rough as when she first awoke. There was less blood in her spit, the sores on her body had faded into flat stains on her skin, and her scent was less putrid. She was strong enough to limp around the cave and wander outside, where she hunted larger animals and roasted them over a fire. Although the damage to her magical abilities was far from healed, she continued executing vision spells to learn about the state of the coven.

The spells used up all her energy, but she had to know more.

In one of her sessions, she saw Jasmyn, Patricia, and Regina defeat the great Foreman Clan in a tremendous battle, with an enormous red dragon at their side. She felt pride at their victory, but it was short-lived—her resentment quickly took over.

"Why hasn't she come for me? I could have helped. I could have been a part of that victory." She turned to her skull council. "Have I not served my sentence? Am I not forgiven? We are still coven sisters, after all, are we not?"

A few more days passed and Loritida's physical strength slowly improved. After another vision spell that produced no new information, Loritida decided to concentrate on her healing. Instead of using her energy on magic, she hunted for larger, more nourishing food.

Now, she sits on her bed and feasts on an arctic tern, trying to solve this puzzle.

"I don't understand it." Loritida bites into the wing. "Jasmyn is Finna's kin. She inherited all her memories and magic, including her blood spells. She freed me. So, why hasn't she come for me? She knows exactly where I am. She sent me here!"

She turns to her skull council, but they remain still and silent.

With a loud gulp, Loritida swallows the meat and throws the wing bones onto a pile of bones in the corner of the cave. She picks up the other roasted wing.

"Do you think she's still mourning her siblings' deaths?" she asks the first wolf skull. "Maybe she wants me to go to her." She huffs. "I have just enough strength to hunt, but I can't navigate these seas alone. I don't even have a ship!"

Without any new ideas from her skull council, she throws her food against the wall and storms out of her cave. She searches the fresh blanket of snow for something large to throw, something enormous to destroy, but finds nothing. She screams into the air and waves her arms frantically, stomping her feet, releasing all her frustration. Light snow flurries around her as she trudges to the edge of the icy cliff.

"Haven't I suffered long enough?" she shouts at the top of her lungs. "Haven't I served my sentence? What are you waiting for? Why haven't you come for me? Why release me from my hold and leave me here?" She inhales deeply and shouts once more, "Why are you doing this to me?"

She drops to her knees and whimpers, "Why?"

After a silent minute, an icy but gentle breeze blows against her, and she hears a whisper. She gasps as the words become clearer, as Joseph Tiller's voice becomes stronger. She immediately recognizes the spell Ryland taught her so many years ago.

And as soon as she grabs hold of Joseph's voice, she drops to her knees and uses all her strength to put him under her spell. As soon as the spell ends, she falls to the ground, closes her eyes, and breathes deeply as her body sinks slowly into unconsciousness.

Ryland, of all people, how could I have forgotten about you . . .

5

FORGOTTEN

In the last room of the top floor of a small hospital for unidentified coma patients, a strong gust of enchanted northern wind flows in through an open window, carrying a spell that wakes Doramae from her sleep. She opens her eyes, sits straight up in her bed, and gasps for air.

After her eyes adjust to the dim hospital light, she inhales and releases a deafening scream. Once all the air flows out of her chest, she covers her face and sobs silently.

After so much time, after so many centuries, why give me back my memories now?

Ever since she awoke on a snowy hill on a desolate island centuries ago, Doramae was oblivious to her identity. She had no memory of her coven sisters or of the years spent living on the Isle of Enid. Her memory was wiped clean.

Scared and confused, she learned to survive in the wild. She lived on the island for decades before modern exploration expanded northward and she found her way off the archipelago and into modern civilization. She traveled across Europe and lived a simple, quiet life as a painter and sculptor.

Although Doramae didn't understand why she was immortal, she knew full well it was vital that no one know of this universally suspicious trait, so changing her location and identity became routine. She gave up trying to figure out her origin and decided to live in the moment. For the most part, she was content with her life as she knew it.

Doramae was standing in line in an art supply store in London to purchase supplies for a personal commission the moment Agatha took her last breath. A jolt of electricity coursed through her entire body, shaking her to her core. The memories of her life rushed in like a merciless tsunami—her entire childhood, her family's sorcery, the love of her coven sisters, the sorrows of wars, and the crimes she committed that led to her being sentenced to the Forgotten Existence. She recalled the exact moment Finna executed the spell that sent her to that remote island without an idea of who she was.

Doramae was so utterly overwhelmed by misery and rage that her heart rate spiked, and she fell to her hands and knees and fainted. She hit her head hard on the floor and fell into a coma.

Now, she sits in her hospital bed, remembering her life on the Isle of Enid. Tears stream down her cheeks as she laments how much time has passed since Finna entrapped her in a blood spell.

All those years alone, not knowing who I was or why I was there. You just left me there to . . . I couldn't even die!

Her heart aches as she recalls jumping off a cliff into the icy sea, only to survive and suffer more anguish. Attempted drownings and tumbles down jagged mountains proved ineffective against the immortality that kept her from committing suicide. She couldn't understand why she was cursed to live alone on the deserted archipelago.

And now you're giving me back my memories? Why now, Finna? For what purpose? I thought you were fair and just. I never thought you'd be this cruel.

After she replays the last few moments with her coven, just before Finna cast the blood spell that would wipe her knowledge of the coven's existence from her memory and send her to the remote island chain in the North Atlantic, she recalls the dreadful sentence they gave her husband.

Her eyes widen. "Moran!"

Blood oozes onto her hospital gown when she yanks the intravenous tube from her arm. She shifts to the edge of the bed, drags her numb legs over the edge, and pushes herself off. She stifles her cry when she lands on her side on the hospital floor, her legs having atrophied from her coma these last few weeks.

She slithers to the bathroom, closes the door, and props her tall body in a seated position against the wall next to the sink. She reaches up to turn on the faucet and fills a bedpan with water. Once it's full, she lowers it to her lap, then pulls down the front of her hospital gown to expose the enchanted tattoo she and Moran etched right above their hearts.

With her jagged thumbnail, she digs at the tattoo until the skin breaks and blood spills down her chest. She redirects the blood into the water and executes a location spell for her husband.

Nothing appears, and her heart breaks all over again.

She squeezes the cut to produce more blood for another attempt. Still nothing.

She tries once more, her heart beating louder with each failure. After the final attempt, she throws the bedpan across the bathroom floor and screams ferociously. The plastic bin bounces and skids, spilling water and blood everywhere. She picks up the container and stares at its empty contents. Her sobs eventually fade to whimpers, and she sits against the wall, staring at the white floor tiles.

"You let him die," Doramae whispers, her voice hoarse from her screams. "You let Moran die. All we wanted was to be together. All we wanted was to love each other for the rest of our lives."

Moran's smile appears in her mind, and his laughter echoes in her ears. She remembers his tender touch, his passionate kisses, his fierce yet loving stare, and she closes her eyes to revel in the memory of her one and only love.

After a long, deep breath, she opens her eyes. "Only you had the power to give us that gift, Finna. Instead, you killed him. You killed us."

She picks up the plastic bedpan and bends it until it breaks. She takes the jagged edge of plastic and cuts her palm.

As a few droplets of blood splash onto the tile floor, Doramae squeezes her fist, presses her lips together, and whispers, "You will be avenged, Moran. They will all die—Finna, the coven, all of them. I swear to it."

JUST BREATHE

Jasmyn's stomach has never growled and gurgled like this. She's called and texted Regina at least a dozen times to see if she can guide her, but Regina has yet to reply. When she called Patricia and told her the universe was trying to send her a message, Patricia mumbled something long and only vaguely coherent, then ended the call. In between the grunts and curses, Jasmyn understood this much: "Regina is on it ... sleep until three ... call only if emergency."

On the hotel room table, the paper bagel bag taunts her, and she remembers how she teased Brian about the awful bagels in the hospital. She smiles and picks up her phone.

> **Jasmyn**: I have a freshly baked bagel, and I can't eat it. I have an upset stomach. So unfair.
>
> **Brian**: More like sweet, poetic justice. Next time don't tease the less fortunate.
>
> **Brian**: You want to know what's unfair? I have these nodules shooting electricity up my thighs and calves. It's supposed to help, but it hurts like hell.
>
> **Brian**: Is your stomach bad? Do I need to worry?
>
> **Jasmyn**: No. I'm fine. I'll text you later.

She sets her phone on the side table and curls into the fetal position, filling her lungs with air, then blowing out forcefully. She closes her eyes and takes more deep breaths.

What is nature trying to tell her? Is it good news? Bad news? More dragons? Another clan? More death?

After several minutes of tumultuous thoughts, she lies flat on her back and picks up her phone to peruse old text messages. She opens the message thread with her father and, as much as it pains her, she reads it again.

Jasmyn received her father's first text the day Logan's body arrived back home. It was a heartfelt note about how much he loves her and how he's always been so proud of her strength and independence, an outpouring of emotion that left Jasmyn in a puddle of tears.

Days later, her father sent details of Logan's funeral—the peaceful songs sung by their church choir, the serene arrangements of white lilies on Logan's casket, and the beautiful sermon by their family pastor. He included how the entire community has supported them through both Katarina's and Logan's deaths, and how he felt everyone's love and compassion.

Even though she's never replied to a single text, her father has continued to send her messages about what's been going on back home. Letters and food left by neighbors, and even smaller events like a car accident on the highway. She's never sensed a hint of resentment or blame in his messages. She's thankful for that.

After scrolling for a while, she returns to the text her father sent two days ago. Her chest swells, and a single tear flows onto the pillow. She reads it over and over and whimpers.

Dad: Jaz, we miss you. Come home when you are

ready. We'll be here waiting for you. Remember, we love you.

She slams the phone onto the bed, wipes her face clean of tears, and breathes deeply.

She can't talk to her parents. She can't go home and mourn with them. She can't reply to her father's messages. She can't accept their forgiveness or comfort. Accepting it now means accepting Katarina's and Logan's death as immutable facts, and she can't do that.

She's on a mission, and no matter how it ends, she'll never be able to go back home.

With a swipe, she closes her father's messages and stares at her phone's background image—a photo of herself posing with Katarina and Logan at her last birthday dinner. The three of them smiled as their parents instructed for the shot, posing as a happy set of siblings. She stares at the photo for a few seconds before setting an alarm for noon.

Her stomach still aches, but she's getting used to the tightness. She places the phone face down on the bed and closes her eyes, then shakes her head once more to fight off the images of dead bodies that continuously appear in her mind.

"Stop thinking, Jaz," she whispers, taking another deep breath.

"Don't think. Just breathe."

7

A TRIAL

After spending the entire morning hiking the Appalachians in New Jersey, Regina knows nothing more than she did when she woke up. The early afternoon sun warms her cheeks as she drives back to their airport hotel with plenty of time to rest before their flight to Manchester.

The long car ride gives her a chance to review her attempt at communicating with nature. Her fingers brushed against the trees and plants as she hiked to a high peak on the mountain. She cooed at birds, squirrels, and chipmunks whenever they came close, whispered enchantments to thick tree trunks, sang songs of the forest up at the leaves, and performed other techniques to gain nature's trust.

When she reached her summit, she took off her boots, pressing her toes against the cold rock, and allowed the wind to whip her hair away from her face. She whispered her vision spells with her eyes closed, entrusting her surroundings with her own safety, with her own life. She was one with the natural world.

She did everything she's learned, everything she was taught, but nothing worked. She's communicated with the Appalachian Mountains before. Why didn't it work this time?

Maybe Mother Nature has nothing to say to me. Maybe it's all in my head, as Patricia said. Or maybe I should have gone to the higher peak—but that was another hour, and more of a rock climb than a trail hike. I don't have equipment for that. No, that couldn't have been it. I was already high enough. It was cold up there. I felt the mountain wind.

She gasps.

Instead of hiking up into the mountains, maybe I have to go down to the sea!

From the left lane on the highway, she veers right, crossing three lanes. Several cars honk at her abrasive maneuver as she pulls onto the shoulder. She searches on her phone for the nearest beach.

"Over an hour away," she whispers, glancing at the clock. "And it's already 1:20." She steps on the gas and flies down the highway.

The salty sea breeze brushes against her face as she climbs out of the car at the boardwalk on Rockaway Beach. She takes off her boots and socks, rolls up her tights at the ankles, and tucks the bottom of her floral dress into her belt. With bare feet, she runs to the waterline and digs her toes into the wet sand.

Eyes closed, she stretches her arms out to the sides and raises her face to the sky to allow the crisp Atlantic Ocean air to blow freely against her body. The whooshing rhythm of the waves caressing the shore lulls her into a deep state of meditation.

She can feel nature's presence in the air, under her feet, in the blanket of the warm morning sunlight on her face. Her skin tingles as the cold water brushes up against her ankles and she accepts nature's invitation. After a few seconds of complete serenity, a choppy vision appears in her mind, an old memory passed on to her through her mother, Jezebel. She welcomes it, and it moves to the forefront and crystallizes.

In the vision, she sees a woman standing in the middle of a vast meeting house, black hair flowing over her shoulders and down her gray frock. She faces a panel of the five eldest sorceresses of the coven. A crowd of villagers gather behind the woman, behind a long, wooden divider. Regina is looking on from the corner of the room, from where Jezebel sits with the teenage sorceresses of her coven to witness the trial.

"Dark magic is our only solution," Loritida says, a fierce look in her profound blue eyes. She faces the crowd behind her. "Would you rather we all fall victim to the next marauders who find our land? Our village barely survived the last attack." She looks back at the panel, her right hand forming a fist. "It is up to us to protect our land, our people, our own families, by whatever means necessary."

The villagers nod and mumble to each other.

A wooden hammer bangs on the table, and the crowd quiets.

"Dark magic is not a wise means of defense," Finna says, sitting at the center of the council. "You will fall prey to its power, Loritida, and take us all down with you."

"I can control it, as you can plainly see, Finna." Once again, Loritida addresses the crowd. "Did I not protect us from the Korrinders' raid last month? Did we not save our harvest from those marauders? Are your homes not intact even after they attacked us with all their might?"

The people nod.

"And look at me now." Loritida spreads her arms wide and slowly spins in place. "Am I not as collected as before? Do I seem like the unnatural, undead monster that dark magic would transform me into, as Finna wants you to believe? I remain in full control of my senses, and maintain my composure against darkness's influence."

She faces Finna directly and lifts her chin. "We are not all vulnerable to its power. And as your coven leader, I say we should embrace it, use it to our advantage. We should attack these clans and prove to them they can't dominate us. We should dominate them!"

Canes stomp on the ground, and the women and men of the village cheer Loritida's words. Loritida smirks to one side and thanks the villagers for their support.

Finna slams the hammer down, and the people stop their clamoring. Once the hall stills, Finna says, "Loritida, did you not sacrifice one of the villagers to work your dark magic? Ferrel, a young boy with barely a hair on his chin."

Whispers and gasps fill the hall. A moment passes, and Loritida narrows her eyes at Finna. She faces the crowd behind her, softening her expression. "He was an orphan. I made sure to choose someone who would not be missed. Without the sacrifice of this insignificant life, we would all have been slaughtered, every single one of us." She addresses the panel, standing tall and proud. "It was a small price to pay for the safety of our people."

Half the crowd nods, the other half lowers their eyes, displaying neither agreement nor dissent.

Finna slams the hammer again, silencing the mumbles. "And who are you to decide whose life is insignificant? Who will be next? Shall it be the woman in the hooded drape standing there behind you, or that old man with the walking stick, or perhaps the babe in that mother's arms, too young to even have a say in the matter?"

Mumbles stir among the villagers.

Loritida shakes her head. "Sacrifices have to be made in order to provide safety for our people," she shouts at them. "Ferrel's sacrifice should be honored, not demonized!"

Another strike of the hammer silences everyone, and the hall quiets. Finna stands, walks around the table, and scans the crowd, looking directly into the eyes of those courageous enough to meet her stare.

"Self-sacrifice to save our people ... yes, that is honorable. But Ferrel did not choose to sacrifice himself. You chose for him."

Loritida's upper lip twitches. "As your leader, I have to make tough decisions for the good of our people."

"For the good of our people . . . Finna repeats while looking across the crowd. "Wasn't Ferrel one of 'our people'? Wasn't Glasgo, the homeless beggar who babbled about flying cows . . . was he not also part of 'our people'?"

The villagers mumble comments and questions of not having seen Glasgo in a long while.

"That's right. Loritida used Glasgo for her dark magic, and that magic failed, didn't it Loritida?"

Loritida rolls her eyes. "Yes. There will be mistakes. Errors will occur."

"Errors? You mean lives will be lost because you do not have control over dark magic, as you claim."

Finna strides up to Loritida, and they glare at each other before Finna turns again and addresses the villagers. "Dark magic will only work if a life is sacrificed. And when it does not have a life to feed upon, it feeds on the conjurer."

The people in the crowd look at one another, shaking their heads. Whispers flow.

Finna walks back across the room with her hands clasped behind her back. "Loritida claims that she was able to keep the dark magic from consuming her as we all know it can. She alleges that her presence today is proof that she can control its influence."

Finna whirls on Loritida. "These are all lies. The only reason she was not condemned to its torturous fate is because she sacrificed Ferrel and Glasgo. If it weren't for them, the darkness would have consumed her, and she would have taken us all down with her."

Gasps and grumbles roll through the crowd. "Murderer!" someone shouts, and others take up the chant.

41

With her eyes wide and her arms raised, Loritida shouts over the voices, "That raiding party was like none we've ever encountered. We would have all died against their numbers."

"Liar!"

"Ferrel was a child!"

"Murderer!"

"Killer!"

Loritida yells back, "You all saw the raiders. We would not have survived!"

Finna slams the hammer a dozen times. She gazes out over the villagers and waits for them to settle down.

"We have encountered many raiding parties over the decades, and we have fought them off with our own hands, weapons, and the magic that lies deep in the blood of this coven. Loritida used last month's raid as an excuse to practice dark magic, an excuse to put us all at risk. There is no excuse for such recklessness."

Loritida points at Finna. "We would never have survived the Korrinders, and you know it!"

"Neither you nor I can see the future," Finna says gravely. "But I do know this—not one more person will be sacrificed for your desire to make use of dark magic."

She scoffs at Finna's claim. "It is not my *desire*; it is a necessity! The world is replete with conquering clans, and this last raiding party is only a picture of what is to come. We are not strong enough to defend the isle and all our people." She speaks to the villagers. "We need to use dark magic if we are to survive."

As the crowd roars and Loritida tries to soothe them, Finna and the other four sorceresses on the panel hastily discuss the situation. After a few minutes, Finna pounds the hammer once more, and the crowd calms. She stands and addresses the villagers behind Loritida.

"Let us put the question to the people of the village."

Loritida swallows hard and frowns.

"How many of you believe we should choose a life, among one of you, so that we may continue to use dark magic? And that Loritida should be allowed to choose, by her own criteria, the next sacrifice?"

Not a single breath is heard in the vast chamber.

Finna steps past Loritida again. "How many of you believe we are not strong enough, not skilled enough, that we lack the ability to fight off these foreign invaders as we have done for as long as we can remember?"

Several men scowl at the claim, pounding their chests.

"Who here believes we can produce more weapons, and tighten our defenses, and train our young men and women how to defend our land? Our home? Our own kin?"

Women and men nod and boldly shout in agreement.

"Who believes that defending our families and friends with our own lives is a noble and honorable way to live? Or should we cower and scheme, and arbitrarily sacrifice the life of one, or two, or twenty people, the lives of your family and friends, so Loritida can use dark magic as she sees fit?"

The entire crowd roars, and some spit or stomp their feet and canes.

Finna glances from one pair of eyes to the next. She raises her hands and waits for the villagers to quiet.

"We cannot rely on the unpredictable nature of dark magic and its conjurer. It is a fate worse than succumbing to any raiding party."

Whispers of agreement emanate from the people.

Finna shuffles back to the council table. When she sits, she lifts her gaze to meet Loritida's contemptuous glare.

"For choosing to use dark magic against our coven's order

and against the will of the people we live with and protect, we five, the oldest sorceresses of our coven, sentence you to exile."

Loritida scowls and sinks to sit at her own table.

"And we will hold you in exile until you have proven that you see the error of your choices."

Loritida flips her table and charges toward the council. "You cannot exile me."

Finna puts up her hands in preparation for a fight. "You know how our coven works, Loritida."

The villagers scream and shout.

Loritida spins on her toes to face the crowd. "I am your leader. I know how to protect all of you. Without me, you will die!"

All five women stand, and Finna raises her arms in preparation to execute the spell that will trap Loritida on a remote, desolate island in the north.

Loritida's eyes widen in fear, and she shakes her head. "No. You can't. I am your leader!"

Zaria, Loritida's teenage daughter, jumps out from the crowd of villagers and chucks a spear with deadly accuracy at Finna. As soon as the spear flies from her right hand, she throws another with her left—defending her mother's honor and protecting her own right to be the next coven leader.

But, like a jungle cat predicting an attack, Finna jumps out of the way of both spears and fires a burst of light at Zaria that sends her flying to the far side of the meeting house. The spiky rim of a hanging torchlight pierces Zaria's midsection, almost splitting her in half. Zaria sucks in a gasp of air, and then her head slumps forward, her eyes still open, blood spilling over her lips.

"Zaria!" Loritida shouts as she stares at her daughter's lifeless face. Her mouth remains agape, and tears flow down her cheeks.

Screams burst from the crowd as the people stampede out

of the great hall, stepping over and shoving one another. The four sorceresses on the panel, along with Finna, stand and raise their hands to gain physical control of Loritida and her magic. Loritida's sisters and brothers all run toward the sorceresses in an uncoordinated attack. They throw axes, spears, and clubs, fighting with all their might to avenge Zaria's death.

The commotion ends in seconds. The panel of sorceresses annihilate everyone in Loritida's family.

A dark fire seems to grow inside Loritida, and she scowls and curses at Finna. "You killed my daughter," she says in a low, rough voice. Hate beaming from her eyes, she glares at the other sorceresses. "You killed my family."

"*You* did this to them, Loritida. Your family is dead because of your actions." Finna looks up at Zaria's body, still hanging from the torch. "Zaria should not have died because of you." She glances over at the other bodies and whispers a quick prayer under her breath. With a snarl, Finna glares at Loritida. "You sentenced your family to death."

Finna turns away and consults with the other four sorceresses on the panel. After a minute, she returns to Loritida. "Your sentence still stands. In addition to exile, you will no longer bear children, and you and your magic will be trapped on the island without escape."

The sorceresses standing behind the panel all gasp, and a wave of whispers echoes in the chamber.

"You are to be exiled and imprisoned until I see fit to free you. You will no longer put anyone else in jeopardy; you will not kill another soul."

Loritida does not cry out or make any exclamations. She stands tall and glowers at Finna and the other four women. Finna raises her arm, closes her eyes, and, within seconds, Loritida disappears.

The memory blurs away, and Regina's mind is flooded with the sight of an unfamiliar blonde, Viking-like woman standing on a cliff. The woman turns her head and looks straight at Regina, as if staring into her eyes.

Regina gasps and awakens from her trance.

Without warning, a tall wave crashes into her, knocking her down.

"What the hell!"

Seawater flows from the top of her hair to the ground and back toward the ocean. Another wave approaches.

Regina rushes to her feet and runs up the hill to dry sand where the water can't reach her. This wave crashes closer than the last one, and Regina inches backward. A flock of seagulls flies down to the sand, squawking fervently and flapping their wings at Regina. They block her path to the ocean.

"Okay, okay, no more. Got it. Geez, you didn't have to kick me out of the waves." Regina squeezes excess water out of her dress, and the seagulls all squawk in unison. "Alright. I'm leaving."

Never has nature been so abrupt in ending her visions, but Regina doesn't protest. She curses and grumbles as she storms back toward the boardwalk. After she's far enough away, she turns around and shouts at the water, "Now I know why my mother used to say, 'Mother Nature can be a bitch!'"

8

FORESIGHT

Patricia isn't used to sleeping until three in the afternoon, but after spending the last few nights battling insomnia, she had no choice. Her mind and her body forced her to sleep. Even the most powerful of sorceresses must rest, especially the day before she starts a journey.

The faint buzzing of her phone awakens her, and she answers in a groggy voice, "I'm up."

"Good," Jasmyn says over the call. "Feel better?"

"Yes." She rubs her eyes.

"The last time we spoke, you were a bit scary."

"Sorry. Lack of sleep makes me irritable. I was up until three in the morning again."

"Well, I'm outside your door. I got fresh coffee from the café in the lobby. The receptionist says they make good coffee. And I snagged the last banana-nut muffins."

"I'll be right there," she mumbles. "Give me a sec."

After stretching her legs and arms, Patricia sits on the edge of the bed and twists at the waist to stretch her midsection. The bed creaks when she stands. She walks to the window to pull back the blackout curtains, and the brightness of the daylight makes her squint. When she turns to shield her eyes, she spots the black fleece sweater Gustavo lent her draped over a chair. She takes in a whiff of his scent, puts it on, zips it up, and heads to the door.

"Wow," Jasmyn says when Patricia opens the door. "I

don't think I've seen you so disheveled before."

"Yeah." Patricia turns around and leads Jasmyn to the suite's kitchenette. "I don't know why I'm having so much trouble sleeping these past few days. My thoughts just go . . ." She swirls both her index fingers in circles by her ears.

Jasmyn places the tray of travel mugs and the bag of muffins on the counter. "Your insomnia, Regina's nausea, my stomach cramps . . . the universe is definitely trying to tell us something."

Patricia takes a bit of the muffin and moans with delight. "This is a good muffin. You don't want one?"

After a loud stomach gurgle, Jasmyn burps and covers her mouth. "Sorry. I tried eating a bagel earlier, but my stomach is just in knots. And it tasted like sandpaper. I had to spit it out."

"This is really good."

As Patricia finishes her muffin and sips her coffee, her phone rings. She answers the call and places the phone on the table, facing up. "Hey, Regina. We were just talking about you. You're on speaker. Jasmyn's here."

"Jasmyn! Oh my God, I'm so sorry for not getting back to you. I've been a bit busy. It's totally natural to feel sick if nature is trying to communicate with you. I'll show you how to channel that sick feeling into your powers, though I don't have a lot of experience with it the way my mother did. Anyway, sorry about that. We'll catch up on the flight."

"Are you on your way back from Jersey?" Patricia takes another banana-nut muffin out of the bag, bites into it, and rolls her eyes at its deliciousness. She nods silently at Jasmyn and gives her a thumbs-up.

"I'm at a beach, about thirty minutes away."

"The beach?" Patricia's forehead wrinkles. "I thought you went to New Jersey."

"I did, but I saw nothing. On my way back to the hotel, I stopped at a beach. After a few minutes of meditation, I got a vision of Loritida's trial."

Patricia, about to take another bite of her muffin, stops and leans forward in her chair. "Loritida?"

"Yeah. Weird, right?"

"Wasn't Loritida sentenced to exile?" Jasmyn asks. "I read that story in the Book of Whispers a million times over."

After one last drink from her coffee, Patricia stands up and changes her clothes. "Tell us what you saw."

"I saw my mother's memory of the entire trial. Beginning to end. It was crazy. I felt like I was actually there, in that great hall with all the other coven sisters. I was in my mother's shoes, witnessing the whole thing. The angry mob, the accusations, the attacks, and the moment Loritida was finally exiled. My mother's memories were already reduced to hazy glimpses, but I got a full, high-definition version of this specific event. This sick sensation . . . it's definitely got something to do with Loritida."

"Did you see Loritida as she is now?" Patricia asks.

"I did not. However, I did see a giant woman with long blonde hair staring right at me. She was like a tall Viking. It was so weird. Uh-oh."

"What is it?" Patricia steps closer to the phone.

"Hold on . . ."

Jasmyn and Patricia wince at the low belch coming through on Patricia's cell phone. Once Regina stops burping, she clears her throat and returns to the conversation.

"Sorry about that. Patricia, do you have any memories of the trial?"

"I don't. My mother and I weren't there. I heard about it when I returned from an expedition to one of the more remote islands of the northern sea, about a year after. I recall my mother being distraught at the news. She loved Loritida. They grew up together. And when they were older, they trained and fought battles together."

After pulling on a clean shirt, Patricia pauses and wrinkles her forehead. She paces between the window and the bed.

"What is it?" Jasmyn asks Patricia as she watches from the counter.

"Just before we left for the expedition, my mother believed that something had happened to Loritida. Loritida had become a solitary recluse, always angry with everyone. There were rumors of Loritida practicing dark magic, but my mother never believed it. There wasn't any proof."

"At the trial," Regina says, "the coven claimed she sacrificed a boy's life to experiment with dark magic, and Loritida didn't deny it. In fact, she defended her actions. She was found guilty by a committee of the oldest sorceresses. Then Finna used a blood spell to exile her."

"A blood spell?" Patricia stops pacing abruptly.

"Yep," Regina replies.

Patricia closes her eyes for a few seconds, then sighs. She opens her eyes and stands by the window, staring off into the blue afternoon sky.

"What?" Jasmyn asks from the counter. "What is it?"

"Finna used a blood spell to exile Loritida," Patricia says, still staring outside. "Blood spells can only be undone by the caster. And, if the caster dies, the ownership of the spell is passed on to the successor." She turns to face Jasmyn. "But, with Agatha, there was no clear successor."

Jasmyn swallows hard. "So, the blood spell is broken."

"Right. Loritida is free." Regina groans. "That must be why I got this vision." She burps once more and clears her throat again. "Guys, I have to go. I think I'm about to hurl."

Over the call, Jasmyn and Patricia hear Regina turn off the car engine, swing the driver's door open, and throw up whatever is left in her stomach. Jasmyn shudders at the gross sounds, and Patricia picks up her phone and ends the call.

"This doesn't make sense," Jasmyn says.

"What part?"

"If that's nature's message, why is Regina still sick? Shouldn't she have stopped feeling sick once she figured out the warning?"

Patricia nods. "That's a good point."

"And . . . wouldn't she have been sick since Agatha died? That's when the spell would have been broken, right?"

"Her nausea started this morning. Yours, too. You didn't feel sick until today, right?"

Jasmyn nods.

"It's got to be something else." Patricia pulls her boots on. "Gustavo is going to be here soon to take us to the airport. You should go get ready."

When Jasmyn stands up, she bends over, wraps her right arm around her midsection, and grunts with pain. "I'm fine." She grumbles, stands up straight, and walks out of Patricia's room with short steps. "I'll meet you outside."

9

LEADERSHIP

As they drive to the airport, Patricia brings Gustavo up to date on their revelation. Jasmyn flips through the pages of the Book of Whispers in the back seat, concentrating on the story of Loritida's exile. Although she's read it several dozen times throughout her childhood, she is reading it now with a new perspective, hoping to find new clues. She tries to ignore the conversation in front of her, sinks down in the seat, and immerses herself in the images and text of the ancient book.

"What an incredible story," Gustavo says as he steers the truck past the gate of the airport parking lot. "Is there anything else we need to know about this Loritida character?"

"That's about it." Patricia shrugs her shoulders. "Loritida's trial was like folklore to me. Just another cautionary tale, a warning against using dark magic for selfish means."

"Well, I wouldn't call it selfish." Gustavo turns another corner. "Loritida wanted to preemptively dominate the clans who posed a threat. Kill or be killed. It's not illogical to think that way, especially back then when the world was all about life or death. Using dark magic to defend your people, if you were lucky enough to have it, was probably a good idea."

"Except that the price of using dark magic is human life." Patricia's back straightens. She faces Gustavo squarely. "She was killing the people she claimed she was trying to protect—orphans, lonely old people, derelicts—to practice her magic." She shakes her head. "How can you defend her?"

"I'm not defending her; I'm just saying she wasn't completely crazy. A lot of civilizations throughout history were wiped out by conquerors, and they would have given anything to save their people. They would have sacrificed everything if it meant their people would live. I mean . . . look at your coven. Finna used the time-reversal spell to save her coven. If she had access to dark magic—"

"She did have access." Patricia cuts Gustavo off in a more indignant tone. "We all have access to dark magic. It's available to all of us. Finna decided not to use it because it has detrimental consequences. She chose the higher road."

"Yes, she did," Gustavo shoots back with a glare. "And how has that worked out for the coven?"

Patricia gasps and sits back in her seat, agape.

Gustavo pulls into a parking spot and shuts off the engine.

Jasmyn lifts her eyes from the Book of Whispers but remains quiet in the back seat.

After a few seconds, Patricia crosses her arms and glances out the side window.

"I'm just saying . . ." Gustavo says in a softer tone. "Finna might not have agreed with Loritida's methods, but she agreed with her intentions. Finna and Loritida both wanted to protect their people, whatever the cost." Gustavo places his hand on Patricia's arm. "As the coven leader, I'm sure you understand."

Patricia glares at Gustavo. "I'm not the coven leader."

"Uh, yeah you are," Jasmyn blurts, then shrinks back in her seat. "Sorry, I didn't mean to interrupt."

She turns around and faces Jasmyn. "If anyone's the leader, it's you. You're Agatha's kin."

"Nope." Jasmyn flips the pages of the Book of Whispers and stops at a particular page. "According to the coven's order, the leadership position is automatically handed down to the coven leader's chosen successor upon her death. The only time this doesn't happen is if the coven leader dies without a successor, like Agatha, or if the council of the oldest sisters of the coven unanimously votes to overthrow the current leader, as was the case with Loritida. The coven then votes for the new coven leader." Jasmyn closes the book and sits back in her seat.

"Looks like you're the one," Gustavo says to Patricia.

Patricia rolls her eyes. "No one voted for me to be the leader."

"Oh, please." Jasmyn rolls her eyes at Patricia. "If we held a vote of all the coven sisters right now, which is basically just me and Regina . . . yeah, I think I can safely say you're our new leader." Jasmyn presses her lips together to hold back a smile. "Please don't exile me."

They all chuckle at the joke, and Gustavo reaches for Patricia's arm. She melts into his soft gaze and smiles back at him.

"You know what?" Jasmyn opens the Book of Whispers once more. "You just reminded me of another exile story in here."

"Well, we have a lot of airport security to go through with all the new protocols," Gustavo says as he opens the door. "We should get moving."

"Give me a sec," Jasmyn says while flipping the pages. "I'll be right out."

Patricia and Gustavo both step out of the truck and shut their doors.

"You know," Gustavo says in a mischievous tone as they walk toward the rear. "With leadership comes a lot of responsibility."

"Will you shut up?"

When they meet at the back of the truck, Patricia lifts her right index and middle finger up at Gustavo. "I have two sorceresses in my coven. Two! Not much leadership happening there."

"Just own it." Head tilted, Gustavo steps closer to Patricia. "You're the leader of your coven. It's a good thing. Jasmyn looks up to you. Regina is . . . well . . . Regina. You think they're ready to be leaders?"

A plane flies low to the ground, creating a light gust that brushes up against their bodies as they stand a foot apart. Patricia's eyes are trapped by Gustavo's gaze. She loses herself in the playful moment. His aura embraces hers, calming her, and her eyelids close halfway.

She wishes she had time alone with Gustavo to really get to know him, to just *be* with him, but there never seems to be time. For a brief moment, she imagines a simple life—kissing him, holding hands, making passionate love on Sunday mornings. After so many years alone, running wild and free, all Patricia wants is right in front of her, there for her to take.

And in that fleeting moment, she blinks and acknowledges the irony of their plan.

If they succeed in helping Jasmyn reverse time, their feelings for one another, the love and affection forged through everything that has happened, will not exist in their new reality. And no matter how much she loves Gustavo, the truest love, a kind of love she hasn't felt in centuries, she knows she can't hope for anything more than this moment.

Just like you said. A true leader would risk everything for the survival of her people.

Patricia reaches for the rear door, and Gustavo steps away.

"We have a plane to catch," she says, eyes averted.

10

BLOOD SPELLS

Jasmyn jumps out of the truck and rushes to Patricia, the Book of Whispers in her arms. "That Viking woman Regina mentioned. I think she might be Doramae."

"Who's Doramae?" Patricia pulls her luggage out from the back of the truck.

"She's the other exile story in the Book of Whispers. The very last story in the entire book."

Jasmyn points to a page with a drawing of five women in a circle, a tall blonde standing at the center with her hands in a prayer fold. Burning houses and piles of ashes fill the background.

"I have yet to reach the end of that book," Patricia huffs. She squints at the drawing. "Doramae . . . why don't I remember her?"

Jasmyn reads each line quickly and paraphrases. "It's the other exile story. Doramae encountered a leader of the Scyngar clan, Moran, washed up on the Isle of Enid after his ship sank in an ice storm. Not knowing who he was, her first instinct was to enchant him to be her servant. After some time, they both fell in love. They approached Loritida, who was the coven leader at the time, and asked her to grant them an immortal union."

"Hold on." Patricia raises her hand. "An immortal union? I would *definitely* have memories about an immortal union."

"Is that like a marriage?" Jasmyn asks.

"It's more than just a marriage. Normally, when a man marries a sorceress of our coven, they have children and grow old together, as any mortal couple would. A sorceress's immortality ends with childbirth. But, if they don't have children, they can be granted an immortal union so that the sorceress shares her immortality with her husband. Her magic is also shared— whatever powers she possesses, he would have as well. It's a gift the coven does not take lightly, and it's only granted if the entire coven agrees."

"Ahhh." Jasmyn slowly blinks. "Now it makes sense why it was such a big issue with the coven."

"Did they get their immortal union?" Gustavo finishes stacking their bags on a cart and wheels it toward the entrance. Patricia and Jasmyn follow.

"Nope. It says here that most of the coven didn't approve of the union because Moran was from the Scyngar clan, which was known to conquer lands and kill and rape women and children. They didn't trust Moran. Finna was the most vocal about rejecting the request. She claimed an immortal union would give Moran enough power to overthrow the coven. And since the coven denied them the immortal union, Doramae and Moran later returned to the Scyngar clan and attacked the Isle of Enid with the entire Scyngar Army."

"What?" Patricia stops and raises her eyebrows at Jasmyn. "An attack by the Scyngar Army? Why don't I remember this? I should have at least inherited this memory from my mother."

"Maybe it was before your mother's time?" Jasmyn shrugs.

"Then I would have my grandmother's memories." Patricia starts walking again, her eyebrows furrowed. "Keep reading."

Jasmyn glances at the book. "Doramae used dark magic to merge wolves and bears with Scyngar warriors to create vicious beasts for the battle. But, even so, the coven was victorious. There were no casualties on the Isle of Enid. The leaders of the Scyngar clan were captured and sentenced to death. However, Loritida asked the coven to show mercy to Doramae. She argued for Doramae's true intention, which was to live with her lover for eternity, not the destruction of the coven. She argued that her intention had transformed into a desperate crusade that could have been avoided if the coven had granted her request for the immortal union."

Gustavo nods and tilts his head side to side. "She has a point."

Patricia glares at him.

Jasmyn rolls her eyes. "In the end, the coven agreed not to sentence Doramae to death. They sentenced her to"—Jasmyn finds the spot in the text where she left off— "a Forgotten Existence."

A soft gasp escapes Patricia as chills crawl down her spine. She stops walking. With her mouth agape, she blinks repeatedly, searching for words to express her astonishment.

Jasmyn guides her forward, a questioning expression on her face. Once they reach a bench on the sidewalk, Patricia sits down and takes a few deep breaths.

Jasmyn sits down next to her. "What's a Forgotten Existence?"

Patricia has always believed in the coven's overall good intentions, especially the coven leaders, at least throughout her lifetime. Finna, Agatha—she would risk her life for them as they did for her. Sure, there were some questionable characters among the sisters, but what family doesn't have a little bit of ugliness? When it was time to defend the coven, to protect their homeland, they were all united. They were family.

It makes Patricia sick to her stomach to know that a leader of her coven would exercise such a punishment on a coven sister.

After a few more seconds, Patricia raises her chin, closes her eyes, sighs, and meets Jasmyn's eager gaze.

"The Forgotten Existence is a horrible spell." Patricia clears the knot in her throat before continuing, "The subject lives out her life without knowledge of her past and is forgotten by all who knew her. So, if Doramae never had children, she should still be alive. She is still immortal. She has no knowledge of who she really is, of where she came from, of the coven, our histories, none of it. In addition, the coven has forgotten about her, too. She is as oblivious to us as we are to her." She glances at the floor. "That's why I couldn't remember her, not even through my mother's memories."

"So, Doramae doesn't know who she really is, and anyone who knew her has completely forgotten about her?"

Patricia nods and swallows hard. "Except for the one holding the blood spell. Loritida."

"Well, not exactly." Jasmyn raises her eyebrows.

"All sentences on a coven sister are executed by the coven leader. Loritida was the coven leader at the time."

"Yes, but Loritida was Doramae's cousin. In the story, it says that Loritida begged the council of the five oldest sorceresses to spare Doramae's life. They agreed to sentence her to a Forgotten Existence, but only on the condition that Loritida was not to execute the spell herself. They feared she would release her cousin too quickly. So, Finna was chosen to execute the blood spell instead."

"Finna executed the Forgotten Existence spell on Doramae," Patricia says slowly, closing her eyes as the realization hits her. "And now, that spell is broken too."

Jasmyn shuts the book and sits back on the bench. "My stomachache is gone."

Patricia nods, pulls out her phone, and calls Regina.

"I'm ten minutes from the airport. Told you I'd make it," Regina shouts, then burps. "I threw up all over myself back there. I had to stop at a gas station to clean up and change my clothes." She burps again. "Excuse me. Sorry about that. I'll be there soon."

Patricia grimaces. "I need you to turn around and go back to the beach."

"What? Why?"

"I need you to see if nature will tell you anything about Doramae."

"Doramae? The name sounds vaguely familiar. Oh! I remember! The Forgotten Existence story. I don't *actually* remember Doramae, just the story in the Book of Whispers. But, then again, that's the whole point of the spell, right?"

"The Forgotten Existence was executed by Finna."

"Ah, so maybe her spell's been broken too. Got it. Maybe she's that tall blonde that appeared in my vision just before the wave crashed into me. Okay. I'll see what I can find out. You know, if I go back, I'm definitely missing the flight."

"Regina," Gustavo says as he glances at his phone, "there's a commercial flight in three hours. I think I can get you on it."

"Great! Send me the flight info once you have it. I'm getting off at the next exit."

Patricia nods and sighs. "We'll see you tomorrow."

"Right, Boss Lady. Over and out."

When Regina hangs up, Patricia stares at the screen, mind churning over the details of the story. "The book said something about Doramae merging animals with humans, right?"

Jasmyn nods.

"That's dark magic." A moment passes, and Patricia stares at Jasmyn, worry tugging at her.

Gustavo catches Patricia's gaze. "What does that mean for

us?"

She swallows hard. "It means Doramae and Loritida have no qualms about using dark magic to get what they want. Loritida was a very powerful sorceress, and from the story it seems Doramae was too."

She glances over at Jasmyn, and her throat dries up. Neither Jasmyn nor Regina is ready to go up against such experienced sorceresses.

They will definitely use dark magic. Maybe Jasmyn and Regina can learn enough to defend themselves, maybe even attack Loritida or Doramae if needed. Or maybe . . .

Patricia lowers her gaze and shakes her head.

It's too risky. If either one of them is consumed by the darkness . . .

"Patricia, are you okay?" Jasmyn asks.

Still shaking her head, Patricia glances away and blinks wildly.

There has to be another way.

"Let's just stick to the plan," Gustavo says.

He grabs her arm and lifts her to her feet, drawing her attention back to the moment, keeping her thoughts from spiraling into the void.

"We'll fly to Manchester, see Ryland, head to the Isle of Enid."

Patricia nods and swallows hard as nightmarish visions overrun her thoughts.

Gustavo guides her through the private terminal toward the airport security gate. Patricia floats along, robotically following the orders of the security personnel, opening her bags, and showing them her identification. Once she's through, she follows Gustavo to the boarding ramp. As she climbs the stairs, before stepping into the private jet, she glances up at the twilight sky once more.

Loritida and Doramae . . . what are they up to?

11

MADNESS

In all the years Jack has traveled with Joseph, he has never seen his captain behave so strangely.

Sid and Clark pace and mumble frantically at the front of the boat as Jack leans against the rail, his arms crossed over his peacoat. He studies Joseph and Shawn through the control-room window. They're having a fight. Joseph waves his arms sternly, shakes his head, and shouts at Shawn.

The first mate finally nods and exits the room.

Jack, Sid, and Clark stand tall when Shawn arrives in front of them. "Everything swell, Shawn?" Jack asks.

The first mate takes a deep breath. "We're still headed north, to those coordinates he gave. He says he's sure there's no ice in our way, and we're picking up some woman named Loritida."

"We're rescuing a woman?" Sid's voice squeals higher than normal. He leans in close to the men and lowers his voice. "Out here? This far north?"

"The captain's gone mad," Clark says. The rosary beads he normally wears around his neck are now wrapped around his hand, clutched to his chest.

"Sailing this far north, at this hour"—Sid looks up at the night sky—"and without the proper equipment for ice."

"He assured me there was no ice."

"How does he know, Shawn?" Sid squeaks. He looks over his shoulder. "You know it's crazy. We have to stop him."

Jack, still leaning against the rail, grunts and rubs his neck.

"I wouldn't do that if I were you."

"Why not?" Shawn demands.

"Rán has her claws about him now."

"Oh, quit your fables, old man." Shawn looks out to sea. "There's a logical explanation for this."

Jack snorts. "You're right—I'm old. But you're a fool. If you don't believe in Rán after all that, I don't know what to tell you. Look at the captain." He points to the control-room window. "He's talking to himself right now. Maybe he's talking to her. What was her name again?"

Shawn presses his lips together. "Loritida."

"Well, I won't say 'I told you so,' because it won't help much, but . . . I told you so."

Shawn takes off his hat and slaps it against his leg. "Damn it, Jack, if you can't say anything helpful, then don't say anything at all!"

Jack spits over the rail. "Fine. Maybe this old man has seen this before, ever think of that?"

"Have you?"

The three men stare at Jack intently.

"Aye . . . I've seen men under a witch's spell. The thing is, if you cross him or try to convince him that he should fight the spell, or anything the like, he'll kill you."

They shift back and forth nervously, glancing over their shoulders.

"He's not thinking for himself anymore. She controls him now. So"—Jack rubs his neck again—"I suggest we act as if nothing's happened and just follow his command until we get back to the marina. Then you can all run. I'll make up something."

"You're staying with him? Are you insane?" Sid says. "You don't think he'll kill you too?"

Jack frowns at the three men. "Joseph is like a son to me.

I'm not leaving his side."

They all curse under their breaths and pace the deck in circles.

"Look." Jack shrugs. "You don't have to listen to me, but if you'd listened before, we wouldn't be in this predicament."

"Okay, okay." Shawn gestures for everyone to huddle. They form a circle, and Shawn speaks quietly. "Let's just play along until we get to the marina. Keep busy. I'll try to keep the captain in the control room, and you guys stay out here. Agreed?"

Everyone nods.

Shawn claps his hands. "Sid, Clark, check below and make sure everything is in order. Jack, stay on deck and keep an eye out. Let me know if you see anything."

"Aye," Jack says. As soon as Sid and Clark disappear below, he adds, "What about the captain?"

"I'll be in the control room. If you see anything out there, anything at all, a shooting star, a whale, a . . . sign . . . anything, let me know immediately."

Once Shawn shuts the door to the control room, Jack faces the ocean and places his hands on the rails. He leans forward, gazing out at the calm waves that seem to mock him, as if there hadn't been a supernatural commotion just a few minutes earlier.

The sea breeze conjures up memories of his father, and Jack digs into his shirt to pull out the pendant handed down through his family from generation to generation, dating back at least two centuries. It has hung around his neck ever since he was twelve years old.

His fingers curl around the eight tridents spiking out from the center of the pendant, a relic that has proven its mystical protection over the years, just as his father had promised. Time and time again, Jack has survived shipwrecks, storms, attacks from sea creatures, and even scuffles among crewmen on the various vessels he's traveled upon. He attributes his long seafaring life to the possession of this enchanted charm.

Jack places the pendant between his hands in a prayer fold and closes his eyes.

Father, you've saved me more than I can remember, but now I need your help to save Joseph. Please guide me as you have before. Joseph is like a son to me. Please help me. Help us. I beg of you. Don't let Rán get the best of him.

He kisses the pendant and presses it to his forehead before stuffing it inside his shirt. After straightening his hat and peacoat, he scans the open waters with his binoculars, east and west, then north and south back to Iceland, which is barely in sight. He lowers the binoculars and sighs.

Nothing. Nothing is better than what we just went through. Nothing is a good sign.

12

REGRETS

As the private jet lands at Akureyri Airport in Iceland, Ryland finishes writing his thoughts in his journal, places his pen in the nook, and closes the little book. He shuts his eyes and takes a deep breath as he imagines how Loritida will greet him. Will she be thrilled? Resentful? Angry at him for his absence all these centuries? He huffs and smirks as several scenarios play out in his mind.

Their romance was never simple.

"Why are you smiling, my lord?" Oregon asks.

"I have no clue how Loritida will react. She might be ecstatic, or she might take out all of her anger on me." Ryland slips his journal into the leather satchel by his feet. "I'm concerned but excited. It's making me a little giddy."

Oregon chuckles. "Everything will work out, as it always does, my lord. You will see."

The private jet stops rolling, and Ryland watches patiently as Oregon unbuckles his seat belt and stands to stretch. He twists his torso as a petite stewardess wearing a sharp blue uniform approaches.

"Sir, do you need help down the ramp?" she asks. "I can get someone to assist you."

"No, no. I just need to unfold these old joints. At my age, sitting for this long is a strenuous activity," Oregon says with another chuckle. "Thank you. I can walk down those stairs just fine."

"Well, if you need any assistance, just let me know." She smiles and returns to the front of the small plane.

Watching his oldest and closest friend age hasn't been easy for Ryland. In all his existence, there have been only three people he has been able to call true friends, and Oregon is the only mortal of the three.

Ryland never gave a second thought to how mortals age, of what they go through as their bones and muscles deteriorate, their organs malfunction, until he noticed Oregon having trouble breathing while walking up the stairs a few decades ago. That's when it hit him—Oregon will one day die.

Ryland isn't one to pray in any way to any god, but if there was one out there listening to the pleas of an immortal who has sinned more than a multitude of sinners combined, this spiritual being would hear Ryland beg for Oregon to live to a ripe old age, well past normal mortality, before passing away peacefully in his sleep.

"You must keep with those stretches, Oregon. I need you in top shape."

After another back twist, Oregon sighs. "My lord, if only I could turn back the clock, I would take better care of myself. If I had known I would live this long, I would have exercised more."

Ryland chuckles. "We all have regrets. And the longer you live, the more regrets you have."

"Oh, that depends on how you live your life." His spine crackles as he bends his neck left and right and rolls his shoulders. "If you live an honest and true life, and are a generous and forgiving man, your regrets are few."

After one more stretch toward the ceiling, accompanied by a groan, Oregon sighs and picks up his bag from under his seat. "One regret I do have is not having a child," he says offhandedly.

The wrinkle on Ryland's forehead gives away his surprise.

"Why did you not?"

Oregon pauses and looks to the side. "I guess the desire to have a child came to me too late, not until I officially left the church. I was already an old man, at the age where men become grandfathers." He sighs. "We never know what we might regret until it is too late."

It hurts Ryland to know that such a regret exists in a man who has shown him nothing but kindness, compassion, and understanding. He's never looked upon him as an abomination for his immortality, and he's never judged him for his questionable roles in the stories from his past. Oregon is the epitome of generosity and forgiveness, and he suffers a regret that can never be undone.

"What is your greatest regret, my lord?" Oregon swings the bag over to his stronger left arm.

Ryland chuckles nervously, and he can feel his cheeks burn. "There are too many to choose just one."

"Your biggest regret—the one you would change right now, given the chance. What would it be?"

Ryland grabs his bag, and they head toward the aircraft door. As they walk down the ramp and turn toward the terminal, Ryland tries to come up with an answer to a question no one has ever asked him before.

Oregon's questions have never stunned him like this.

He stops to allow Oregon to catch up. When Oregon reaches him, he looks deep into his friend's wise yet sad eyes and feels a sense of shame.

He swallows hard against the knot in his throat. "Not living an honest life. Not being a generous and forgiving man. I could have done so much for so many people and been remembered in a better way. Instead, I lived in the shadows, in the dark corners throughout time, with no one and nothing by which to be remembered. Yes . . . that is my biggest regret."

Oregon nods, and they reach the terminal.

"Immortal or not," Oregon says, "we all want to be remembered. Your regret is not that different from mine. No one will miss me when I am gone. No one will remember me."

"I will miss you, my friend. I will remember you."

"Thank you, my lord," Oregon huffs and smiles, almost childlike. His face glows bright red. "That gives me a lot of peace. I think it's a universal thing, to want to be remembered. No one likes to be forgotten."

A man wearing a black suit escorts them to their car. As they drive to the meeting location, Ryland remembers Loritida's unmatched beauty. The last time he saw her, she had obsidian strands of silk flowing down her head to her waist, a feature matched by her fair skin and eyes that harmonized with the clear blue sky. Her smile, though sometimes wicked, would beam across rooms full of people and draw every man's attention.

She didn't need magic to enchant men—anyone with good vision was a potential victim.

During her exile, Ryland waited for his visions to disclose her location, but when the visions came, centuries later, he saw a woman with pus-filled flesh, covered in moss and grime, sleeping on an icy cave floor. In the visions, Loritida was a fraction of the woman he remembers, and it gives him shivers to recall those images.

I know you will hate me for not coming sooner, Loritida, but I hope you'll understand why.

He pats the suitcase that holds his valuable possessions, then chuckles.

Who am I kidding? You won't understand a single bit. I just hope you'll give me a chance to explain before you kill me.

13

PROTECTION

The frigid winds of the northern seas give Jack a sense of doom as they head back to Iceland. It took hours longer than expected, navigating icy waters and hiking snowy hills in gear not meant for such extreme weather.

It was a direct path to Loritida's cave, but a treacherous one. Nevertheless, they completed their task, and now they're almost back at the marina.

Loritida sleeps below as Shawn, Sid, and Clark prepare to dock. Shawn walks into the control room first, followed by Jack, who closes the door behind them. They take off their thick black beanies.

Jack moves to the other end of the control room and stares out at the marina. Shawn squeezes his hat as he thinks about what to say.

"We want to talk to you, Captain, before we dock."

"What is it?" Joseph keeps his eyes on his clipboard.

Shawn takes another step closer. "The men and I have decided that . . . we won't be sailing with you later today."

"I know it was a long night, Shawn." He lifts his gaze. "We won't be sailing until Loritida has had a chance to rest and clean up. Ryland has set up lodging for all of us at the Hotel Bergvik. Rest, eat, take the entire day off. Just be back here by five."

"We're not tired. I mean . . . that's not the reason."

The captain sets the clipboard down and glances at Jack,

then Shawn. He crosses his arms and stands tall. "Is it the pay? I'll ask for double the money. I'm certain Ryland will pay it."

"It's not about the money. The men don't care about the pay."

Joseph narrows his eyes. "Then what is it about?"

"Originally, the job was to go out north and read the poem. And we did that. Then you asked us to go rescue that woman, and we did that, too, even though we were highly unprepared for that kind of trek. Nonetheless, we did everything you asked."

Shawn lowers his eyes and swallows hard.

After a quiet moment, Joseph says, "Go on."

"We would do anything for you, Cap. We'd even follow you to the ends of the earth. But . . ." He lifts his gaze and meets Joseph's stare. "We agreed to follow you. We didn't agree to follow her."

Joseph nods. "I see." He faces Jack. "You feel this way too?"

"Aye," Jack huffs. "I feel a load more than just that."

The captain takes a step toward Jack and glares down at him. "If you have something to say, old man, then say it."

"Alright." Jack straightens his spine, lifts his chin, and glares right back at Joseph. "That woman is Rán, a daemon, a monster. She is nothing but a creature meant to suck the life out of you. She has you trapped in her claws, under her spell. She's got you thinking like . . . like . . . an idiot, making crazy decisions like trekking that mountain." He frowns hard. "She'll be the death of you!"

In a heartbeat, Joseph lifts Jack's elderly frame, slams him up against the door, and throws him to the other side of the room. Shawn pulls Joseph back by the arms and yells at him to stop.

Jack rolls to his side and rises to one knee. He groans as he stands up. Never did he believe Joseph would attack him this way.

In all the years they've sailed together, through high tides and low, not once did Joseph ever demonstrate superiority or exert physical power over him. A tightness forms in his chest, and Jack glances away when he senses tears forming.

After holding Joseph back for several seconds, Shawn lets him go and shoves him. "Look at yourself, Cap!" He stands between the two men with his arms up as Jack rises to his feet. "You've been sailing with Jack for more than a decade. Are you really going to fight him now? Over that woman? She isn't worth it. The money isn't worth it! We have to leave her!"

Chest heaving, Joseph looks straight at Shawn, then lowers his gaze to the floor. He takes a step back and turns away. His shoulders slump, and he shakes his head.

"I . . . I can't . . . I can't leave her. I can't let her go. She has something on me." Joseph glances sideways at Shawn. "It's like I want to just serve her. Do whatever she wants. I can't fight it."

Shawn takes a step forward. "You can't go back to her. Jack and I won't let you."

"You don't understand. You can't stop me." He closes his eyes and inhales deeply. "What I mean is"—he glances at both men with sad eyes—"*I* can't stop me."

Jack and Shawn exchange frightened looks.

The radio sounds a message from the marina, but Joseph doesn't move. Shawn steps up to answer the call. Then he places the radio back in its holster on the control desk.

"I regret ever taking this job and dragging all of you down with me," Joseph says, staring at the floor. "All the money in the world isn't worth this."

He shakes his head one last time and stands up tall, his shoulders back, and speaks in a more dominant tone. "When we dock, take the men and go. I'll handle Loritida. She still needs me. She can use me however she wants, but at least none of you will be harmed." He nods at Shawn. "Go tell the men."

Shawn puts on his hat and leaves the control room. Once the door closes, Joseph huffs and faces Jack. "You have to go with them. If anything happens to you, I don't think I can live with myself."

With a nod, Jack steps closer and puts his right arm on Joseph's shoulder.

Joseph grimaces. "Don't make this harder than it already is."

"You're like a son to me, Joseph, and I want to help the only way I can. I want to give you something."

Jack pulls the leather cord with his father's charm over his head and sets it around Joseph's neck, like a father passing on an heirloom to a son. He stuffs the pendant behind Joseph's wool sweater, beneath his undershirt, right onto his chest, and straightens his sweater to make sure it is hidden from sight. He places both hands on Joseph's shoulders and stares at him with intensity.

"You listen to me, Joseph Tiller. This pendant came from my father, and his father before him. It has saved my life a dozen times over. It may be too late to save you from that woman's hold, but this might protect you from whatever's to come. Never take it off. Ever. Forget it's even there." Jack frowns, hard and proud. "Make me this final promise. Swear to me that you will never take it off."

Joseph nods and places his hand over his heart. "I swear to you, old man, I will never take it off."

"Never," Jack grumbles, catching the cry in his throat.

Joseph swallows hard. "Never. I swear."

14

MESSAGES

As the jet leaves the private terminal at JFK, Jasmyn drifts off into another dream about her brother and sister. Her phone buzzes, jolting her awake. She pulls it out of her pocket and smiles when she sees Brian's name.

> **Brian:** I know you made a promise to me, but I can tell when you're not being totally honest. So, if you decide not to contact me when you go back, just remember that I would have loved you even without all the drama. I don't need magic and dragons and end-of-the-world stuff to love you. I love you for your smile, your pain, your big heart, and for the hope I see in your eyes. I think I fell in love with you the second I saw you sleeping in your car, before I knew anything about your family's magic. Just remember that.

Her eyes well up, and she blinks to hold back the tears. Another soft smile crosses her face as she remembers Brian's smile when he woke this morning, all groggy and goofy. Her phone buzzes again.

> **Brian:** And don't forget that I knew you when you were a weird kid. If you tell me everything when you go back, the worst I can imagine

thinking is that you're just a weirder teenager.

And I'll love you anyway.

She sighs, closes her eyes, and imagines a world where she and Brian can be together. Logan and Katarina are safe, and there are no family secrets, no magic, no imminent threats. She huffs and shakes her head.

Such a world will never exist.

With a few taps on her phone, Jasmyn sends Brian a smiley and a heart. She sighs and stuffs her phone back in her pocket.

Patricia, sitting next to her, is already asleep and snoring lightly.

What will Patricia be like when they go back in time? Will she be any different than she is now? Will she look at Jasmyn the same way, or will she label her an angst-filled teenager, like everyone else does?

Will she even be around? What would life be like without Patricia and Regina? Without her coven sisters?

Jasmyn shudders.

As the plane speeds up on the runway, her eyelids grow heavy with sleep, and she thinks about Katarina and Logan. She's been successful at directing her subconscious to produce dreams about her brother and sister using a spell Regina taught her. She envisions Logan and Katarina in her mind and whispers the spell until, a few seconds later, she is asleep and dreaming.

~ ~ ~

Logan and Katarina stand atop a mountain peak overlooking a crystal-blue ocean, staring longingly at dragons whisking by in playful flight. Katarina wears her white, lacy dress that dances in the breeze, with daisies in her auburn hair and bangs hanging just above the rim of her glasses. Barefoot in the grass, she spins, occasionally picking up a stone and tossing it for the dragons to catch.

Logan, also barefoot, in his blue jeans and white T-shirt, throws stones farther and harder, presenting a bigger challenge for the dragons. He laughs when Katarina flops clumsily on her side.

When Jasmyn giggles from behind them, they both turn to her with a look of surprise on their faces.

Katarina jumps into a sprint. "We've been waiting for you!"

"Jaz!" Logan waves, smiling. "Come here!"

The dragons halt, flapping their magnificent wings slowly to maintain their position, staring curiously at the visitor. Seconds later, the dragons return to soaring across the sky in graceful dips and dives.

Katarina hugs Jasmyn at her waist, burying her head in her chest. At this exact moment, Jasmyn promises herself, if given the chance, she will hug them more. She will never brush their affection away like she used to, and she will make sure they know, without a doubt, that she loves them.

When Jasmyn pulls away, Katarina runs back to Logan, attempts another powerful throw, and falls once more, groaning. "Show me how to throw farther, Logan."

"It's all in the shoulders." Logan stretches his right arm back as if taking a book off the top shelf of a bookcase. "Start with your arm like this." He steps forward with his left leg, and his right arm follows through. "And then you swing it forward like this."

"Jaz!" Katarina shouts. "Come throw rocks with us!"

Jasmyn picks up a rock and joins them at the cliff's edge. She throws hard to closely match her brother's strength, and at the same time encourages Katarina to keep trying. Hearing her little sister's joyful giggles as she fumbles her throws gives Jasmyn a warm feeling in the middle of her chest, and she smiles so wide her cheeks hurt.

She pauses and takes in the picturesque scene, the shimmering sea, and the baby-blue sky littered with dragons cutting through cottony clouds. More giggles accompany the soft shushing of bushes and tree branches that dance with the ocean breeze—the sound of peace and tranquility.

As she stares all around at the wondrous dream, she drops her rock, lowers her arms, and wonders if their life would have been this happy if none of the events of the past few weeks had occurred.

Could they ever have been this happy?

A frown slowly replaces Jasmyn's smile—their lives would have been nothing like this. She was a jealous, bitter person who left wreckage in her wake. A wave of sadness and pain shatter the moment of pure happiness. She steps back, away from Logan and Katarina, who are oblivious to the change in her demeanor, and leans on a rock to watch her brother and sister from afar.

The awkward flight of a young yellow dragon captures her attention. The dragon's oversized crystal-blue eyes stand out from this distance. The lack of grace and elegance in its flight makes her wonder if it's sick or hurt. Maybe it's younger than she realizes and still learning the mechanics of flying. Maybe it's a clumsy dragon, just as there are clumsy people.

She is mesmerized by the creature as it dives toward the cliff. It flaps its wings in an uncoordinated fashion, breathing forcefully as if straining. She glances over at Katarina and Logan, who remain unaware of this oddity in the sky. When she looks back at the dragon, she watches it zigzag toward the cliff's edge. The movements are so comical that she chuckles.

But as the dragon gets closer, the beast's crooked flight

path suddenly becomes sharp and its wings flap with strength and purpose. It inhales a lungful of air in preparation to blow fire.

Jasmyn immediately raises her arms, her fingers in a claw formation, and executes the shielding spell just in time to stop the blaze from hitting her. Her shield deflects the fire to the foliage around her, and soon her peaceful scene is transformed into an inferno.

The stream of fire doesn't stop. She shouts for Katarina and Logan as the force of the blaze pushes against her enchanted armor. It slowly penetrates her shield and scalds her skin, and she screams in terror.

A shiver travels throughout her entire body, and she wakes up in a cold sweat, panting frantically. She holds her breath for a few seconds, then releases it and repeats a breathing exercise to keep from hyperventilating. She inspects her arms for burns and finds them unscathed.

This dream is unlike the last few she's crafted, of a peaceful pastime with her siblings that ends with hugs and longing goodbyes. This dream was dark and dreadful, out of her control. The real-life memories of Logan's and Katarina's deaths appear in her mind. Jasmyn recalls Katarina's last whimpers as she dies in her arms, and Logan's final scream when the knife pierces his heart.

She takes ten long, slow, deep breaths before the images and sounds fade away.

Regina's words echo in her head. "Sometimes, dark dreams are omens. The universe might be trying to send you a message. Analyze the dream. Focus on the details."

What does it mean?

She lifts the shade and stares into the black night. *What are you trying to tell me? Is there a yellow dragon after me? Does the yellow dragon represent something? Is it Loritida or Doramae?*

After several minutes without coming to a definite conclusion, Jasmyn yawns. She chuckles when she remembers the rest of Regina's advice about dark dreams. "And sometimes, dark dreams are just nightmares, and nothing more, so just let them go."

It was just a nightmare. Let it go. People have dark dreams all the time.

After looking at the time and realizing they're not even halfway to their destination, she adjusts herself in her seat and closes her eyes.

Just a dream. Just a dream.

She repeats her mantra more than two dozen times before her mind relaxes enough to fall asleep.

But, deep down, in the core of all that she knows, of all she's been through, Jasmyn knows it's never *just* a dream.

~ 15 ~

A MORTAL UNION

The overnight hours Doramae sits in the hospital bathroom regaining strength in her legs seem endless, but once she's able to stand, she sneaks through the facility, snatching up clothing and cash from other abandoned people in the nursing home. Once she's fully dressed, she walks past the sleeping security guard and out the front door. The rising sun shines directly in her face as she strides over to a map at a bus stop, then heads to the London Underground.

An hour later, she arrives at her apartment and opens the front door with the key she hid under a decorative garden statue. She rushes to the closet in her bedroom and pulls out a set of plastic containers stacked on top of each other. The black metal picture frame of a project she worked on decades ago sticks out from under a beige cloth. She slides her artwork out of the closet and places it flat on her bed.

In the seventies, Doramac joined a troupe of artists protesting imperialism, corporate greed, and big government. This collage of business cards Doramae created was a statement of how the corporate world was killing mankind. Every single business card she could get her hands on, she placed on this board, then covered the entire collage with thin lines of red paint she characterized as blood money.

One by one, she inspects the hundreds of business cards to find the exact one she's looking for. She pulls out all the black cards—one for a bank, another for a men's tailor, one for a liquor store, and another for a shoe repair—and tosses all of them to the side. Halfway down the board, she sees another black card, mostly buried beneath two yellow cards. She digs and pulls the black card off the collage.

"Yes!"

Way back when she received this specific business card, she didn't think anything of it. She was in the middle of a spiritual getaway in the country with over a hundred participants. Everyone was handing out paper paraphernalia about loving nature, uniting everyone, universal peace, joy, and happiness. The man's long white hair glistened in the sun when he approached her picnic blanket. He smiled, handed her the black business card, and said, "Contact me when you're ready."

When she read the card, she giggled, rolled her eyes, and stuffed it in her bag for her collection.

Now, her heart races as the card Ryland gave her sits in her hand. She didn't know who he was then, but she knows exactly who he is now.

She reads the handwritten message she'd thought was some sort of hippie mantra. "When you realize who you truly are, reach out to me. I will help you find your way."

When she flips the card, she sees his address. She glances at her watch and pulls out her phone to search for the next train to Manchester.

After a hot shower to wash out weeks-worth of oil buildup in her platinum blonde waves, Doramae stands wrapped in her bath towel in front of her mirror, inspecting the raw flesh wound over the tattoo. She lays down on her bed, closes her eyes, and recalls every single detail of the last night she spent with Moran—details so clear it feels like yesterday.

"You were the most brutish man I had ever seen," Doramae says with a chuckle, leaning on her elbows, looking down upon Moran's face as they both lie naked in bed. "If I had not enchanted you when you washed ashore, you would have killed me for sure."

"We Scyngars are not as barbaric as you believe. Sure, we conquer lands like all other clans, but your beauty alone would have enchanted me. You didn't need to use magic."

"It was a precaution." She combs his long hair back away from his forehead. "I couldn't even see your eyes beyond that ragged hair and beard. You might as well have been a monster."

Moran grabs her waist and playfully rubs his nose into her neck, growling. "And now . . . do you still think me a monster?"

"Stop that!" she cries with a laugh. "We need to rest. We have to be up at dawn tomorrow to go over the battle plans with the clan leaders."

After a slight grumble, Moran rolls onto his back. "Are you sure you want to go through with this? My clan leaders agreed to help you defend your claim against your coven, but . . . arriving at the Isle of Enid with the Scyngar Army looks like a raid. If they attack us, which I'm almost certain they will, we will have to fight back. The battle could get ugly. Many of your sisters will die."

"They are no longer my sisters." Doramae covers her body and tightens the blanket at her sides.

"Doramae . . ." His voice turns coaxing. "I love a good battle as much as any Scyngar, but these women are your family. What about Loritida? She's your cousin."

"Distant cousin. Multiple times removed."

He rolls his eyes. "Still, she is your family, and you will force her to stand against you. You yourself have said the women of your coven are like sisters. If we get into a battle and win, you might lose your entire family."

After propping herself up on one arm, Doramae looks down at Moran and smirks. "You have become weak for a Scyngar.

Do I need to look for another husband?"

"Your beauty could weaken the most gruesome of Scyngar men. Regardless . . . there is still time to change our plans. We can find another way."

The bed creaks when Doramae flips onto her back. "There is no other way! I will not go on existing forever while you age and die. Attacking the coven is the only way for us to be together forever."

After a silent second, Moran faces Doramae. "I lost all three of my brothers and all my nephews in our last conquest. Although it's been five years, I still suffer the loss." He swallows hard. "I cannot imagine what I would do if I lost all of my people, all of my family. If we eliminate the entire coven—"

"They're not giving me a choice."

Doramae inhales a lungful of air and blows it out slowly. She swallows, quickly reviews her limited options, then closes her eyes and shakes her head, wishing for another way.

"I don't want to eliminate the entire coven," she says. "I just want to show them how far I am willing to go to be granted an immortal union with you. Loritida will negotiate to avoid an ugly battle. She'll convince the dissenting women to grant us the union in exchange for leaving peacefully."

"And if they don't agree?"

"Then . . . I must kill the dissenters one by one until I get the unanimous vote to grant the immortal union."

When Moran lowers his gaze, Doramae sits up and places both her hands on his cheeks. "I will kill them all if I must. I love you, and I want you to live with me forever."

After gazing deeply into her eyes, Moran nods and pulls away. "You know how else we can be together until the end?"

Doramae raises her eyebrows.

"Let's have a child."

She rolls her eyes, lies back down, and groans.

"We would age and grow old together and have our own family and—"

"No, we won't!" Doramae slaps the bed with both hands and sits up. "Do I have to remind you that my mother died giving birth to a stillborn? She had five stillbirths before she had me, and then one more that killed her. My grandmother had three stillbirths before she gave birth to my mother, and then one more that finally killed her! My grandmother's sister died after a stillborn from her first and only pregnancy. It is a curse on the women of my family."

"I've spoken to our seer, and he says—"

She pounds her fist on the bed. "I don't care what he says! I'm not risking my life!"

Moran rolls onto his back and sighs, staring up at the ceiling.

"I want us to be together until the end of time," Doramae says in a softer tone. She presses her lips to keep them from trembling. "Is that so wrong?"

He turns once more toward the edge of the bed, away from Doramae. She stares at him for several breaths, then places her hand on his shoulder. "My love, if a family is what you truly want . . ."

The bed shakes when Moran shifts completely around. He looks deep into Doramae's eyes. "All I want is you! I love you, and only you. But if we attack the coven and win, and possibly kill all your sisters to get the immortal union . . ."

He pauses, then kneels on top of the covers, raising his eyes to meet Doramae's sad stare. "Killing your family and all your people is a high price. I fear you will resent me for the rest of our existence. And if we lose, then we die. Don't you see? No matter the outcome, we lose."

The sincerity in his voice brings tears to Doramae's eyes.

She presses her lips together as she considers his fears, but it doesn't change her mind. He is worried, so she must find a way to ease his anxiety.

After a few more silent seconds, Moran leans into Doramae and whispers desperately, "The seer said that you are ripe to bear children. If you choose to, you can be a mother—"

She shakes her head and lowers her gaze.

"And that you could have many children with his help and that of the healers. You only need to choose to have children. He has seen it."

Doramae stalks to a chair where her clothes lie in a pile. "You know what I've seen? I saw my mother's face turn blue and her eyes flip back inside her head when she gave birth to that dead child. Did your seer see *that* in his visions? My mother and father had me pray to five graves while my mother was pregnant. Five! We all begged the gods to spare her child, to spare her life!"

She pulls on her frock and stares blankly at the wall for several seconds before turning around to look at Moran. "We had healers perform rituals that were supposed to save her, and we sacrificed countless animals to the gods. Nothing worked. None of it. And our seers . . . they didn't see death in her last pregnancy."

Doramae chuckles devilishly as she puts on her shoes. "The seers could not even see her and her baby die! They can't see everything, and I will certainly not live my life based on what your seers say."

She frowns at the ground and shakes her head. "I still resent my father for convincing my mother to have more children, for trusting our seers, for promising me that she would be fine, that she would not suffer my grandmother's fate." She points at her chest. "I know what resentment is, and I would never resent you. I would count every single day with you as a blessing from the gods."

Moran lies back down, covering himself with the quilt.

After one more drawn-out sigh, she climbs into bed and nudges him to face her. She gazes into his eyes forgivingly. "My love . . . if you truly want a family, then perhaps I should leave. I cannot give you what you want. I will never have children. I will not end my life willingly."

She fights back a sob, and her lip trembles. "I don't want my mother and my grandmother to have suffered for nothing. I must live on, if only for them. They sacrificed their lives for me, to give me life. I must live on, for them."

Moran looks at Doramae, his eyes red. "I want you. You and only you. I don't need a family to be happy. I don't need immortality. Just you. Forever or in death, until the end, I only want you."

Doramae returns his longing gaze for several breaths as tears stream down her cheeks. She sees the honesty in his eyes. She knows in her heart that this is the only path to happiness.

"Let's get to sleep. Tomorrow, we set sail for the Isle of Enid." Moran pulls Doramae into his arms. "If Finna is as reasonable and compassionate as you say, perhaps you can appeal to her emotions the way you have with me. Then she can sway the vote without shedding any blood."

With her head buried in Moran's chest, Doramae sighs. "I doubt it."

"If someone like you can fall in love with a barbarian like me, anything is possible."

A honk from the street brings Doramae back to her apartment. She stares up at her ceiling, tears flowing.

Oh, Moran, how we overestimated Finna's compassion. She would never have allowed a Scyngar to live forever, no matter what we did. Her hatred of your people was too much for any change of heart.

She wipes her tears, sits up, and reaches for her phone on the nightstand. She double-checks her train's departure time, puts down her phone, and packs a bag. After wandering aimlessly for centuries, not knowing where she came from or where she was destined to go, Doramae is content with her new sense of purpose, her new destiny.

Doramae will annihilate the coven, and Ryland will help her find the way.

16

VERMIN

Although they've traveled halfway around the world, the flight did not provide enough rest for Patricia. The lack of sleep the last few nights and the jet lag have left her feeling sluggish. After she and Jasmyn drop off their bags at the hotel room, she stops at the lobby coffee shop and gets two double espressos.

"There!" Jasmyn points at a map of Manchester on her phone. She places her finger on two intersecting streets. "That's where Ryland lives."

"You're sure?"

"Yes, just off the corner. It's clear in the memories I've inherited from Caderyn. This is where we'll find Ryland. It's only ten blocks away."

"Great." Patricia shoots back the last few drops of the first espresso and sighs with satisfaction. She picks up the second cup.

"That's a lot of caffeine," Jasmyn says. "Didn't you sleep on the plane?"

"It wasn't enough, but these will help." She tilts her head back to finish the hot drink, then wipes her mouth. "Let's go."

After a brisk walk, Patricia leads Jasmyn down the narrow alley littered with dead rodents and eager roaches and flies. Dirty water collected from the overnight rain runs along grooves in the walkway, flowing over and around rotting vermin. The daylight exposes the black-and-green grime on the stone sidewalls.

"Watch your step."

Both Jasmyn and Patricia cover their noses at the putrid

smell that greets them at the large hickory door. Patricia gives the door a nudge, and it swings open, creaking loudly and continuously until it hits the wall, as if announcing their presence. An even stronger stench invades their nostrils, and they cough repeatedly as they make their way down the spiral staircase.

Patricia flicks her wrist, whispers a spell, and shoots a tiny flame to a torch hanging on the wall. She lifts it off its handle and hands it to Jasmyn.

"This will help with the smell."

She grabs another torch and proceeds down the steps.

The stone-brick pattern on the walls continues all the way down to the main floor, reminiscent of the dungeons she has visited throughout Europe where people were tortured and killed. The hairs on her arms stand up, and she shifts the torch to her left hand to keep her dominant hand free.

A large rat scurries in front of Patricia's feet, and both Patricia and Jasmyn freeze. The rat skitters down the steps and away into the darkness.

Patricia shivers. "I hate rats."

At the bottom of the staircase, she lights three torches, illuminating the underground chamber.

"Ugh." She winces when she sees a pile of muck covered by a blanket of maggots in the middle of the room.

Jasmyn coughs. "Is that . . . a body?"

"Maybe." Patricia picks up a few pieces of a broken chair, engulfs them in flames, and tosses them onto the pile. With a twist of her hand, she generates a whirlwind that lifts the smoke and stench up and out the door of the chamber. "That should clear up the smell a bit."

Jasmyn lowers her hand from her face. "Yeah, that helped. What are we looking for?"

"Personal possessions, like a watch, a pen, anything

Ryland might have owned or carried on him. Vision spells work on things a person was attached to, including photographs and writings."

As Jasmyn moves toward the left side of the chamber, Patricia goes right.

The quick patter of tiny feet tells Jasmyn the rat is nearby, and she shivers at the thought of it biting her ankles. She holds the torch low to illuminate the floor, but she doesn't see the critter. As she moves about the room, she raises the fire to look at the dusty stone walls, three desks with empty drawers pulled out, and bookshelves clear of any books.

Jasmyn grows accustomed to the scratching sound of the rat's nails trailing behind her, and she casually swings the torch in a circular motion around her legs. The irritating sound stops, but then starts again. She repeats the motion while searching through the bare furniture.

At another corner of the room, a faint light glows around a set of wooden shutters. Jasmyn swings open the shutters, and the sunlight blinds her. She squints and looks away, back toward the blaze in the center of the chamber. Once her eyes adjust to the streams of daylight, she looks out the broken glass window at a slope. At the bottom is a plaza with a fountain of a goddess gazing up at the heavens.

"This dungeon has a really nice view," Jasmyn calls to Patricia. "There's a plaza down there."

"Keep looking," Patricia shouts from afar.

The rat squeals as it jumps onto the windowsill. Jasmyn steps back and gasps. The creature sniffs around the edges of the metal windowpane, back and forth, then jumps down to the floor and scurries under a desk.

"Freaking rat!" Jasmyn swings the torch down by the foot of the bookshelf. She can hear the miniscule animal scratching at something.

"Did you find anything?" Patricia walks back to the center of the room, her footsteps echoing.

"Nothing."

"He cleaned out this place pretty good."

"Do you think he knew we were coming?"

"Possibly. Ryland is a seer. He has visions of things that have happened in the past, and of events that are about to happen. He might have seen us coming."

"But why would he run? I mean, we don't want to kill him, we just want the Book of Sol to see if it has details of the time-reversal spell. Wouldn't he have seen that in his visions?"

"Maybe, maybe not. Either way, it's clear he wasn't leaving anything behind for us to use to locate him."

"Weren't Ryland and Loritida lovers when she was banished? Could he be with Loritida now? Could he be out to rescue her from her exile?"

"Maybe. It's possible he knows about the broken blood spells." A continuous scratching sound catches Patricia's attention, and she bends down in search of the source.

"It's just a rat looking for food. It's been following me." Jasmyn waves the torch low by her feet and the rat hides.

Patricia glances up sharply. "Has it, now?"

Patricia bends pulls a bag of nuts from her jacket pocket. She puts a peanut on the floor to draw the rat out and waits there, staring at the bottom of the bookcase.

"What are you doing?" Jasmyn asks.

"Shh!"

After a few seconds, the rat sniffs its way to the peanut, and Patricia snatches up the dirty creature in her hands. She lifts the rat close to her face, looks right into its tiny black eyes, and whispers, "Are you a rat? Hmm?" She spins the animal in her hands, studying its front and hind feet, twirling its tail around her finger, then returns to gripping it tight. "You're not a rat, are you? Show me who you are."

The rat wriggles and squeals in her hand, and she tightens her grip, keeping it still. "Where are you?" she says, walking across the room and running up the stairs. She shouts at the rat, "Where are you?"

The rat stops squealing, and its head hangs lifeless.

Patricia throws the rat aside, runs past the chamber door, and steps into the bug-infested water in the alley. She catches a glimpse of a tall blonde woman at the entrance of the alleyway just as she turns the corner and vanishes from view.

Jasmyn steps into the alley behind Patricia. "Was that—"

"Doramae." She looks back at Jasmyn. "Don't follow me."

Patricia leaps into a sprint.

Doramae can only run as fast as her weak legs allow, and she can sense Patricia catching up. As Patricia gets closer, Doramae zips across the street, past an oncoming Manchester Metrolink tram that cuts Patricia off.

Patricia waits for the slow-moving tram to pass and follows Doramae into a city park.

Nearly out of breath, Doramae runs past pedestrians walking their dogs, couples strolling down paved pathways, and parents pushing strollers. She follows the train of mothers toward a playground. When she turns to look at Patricia, she stumbles backward onto the ground but quickly rises to her feet. She bumps her head on a low-hanging branch and hides behind a tree.

Doramae isn't ready for a confrontation with a sorceress. Although she's still physically weak, her mental abilities are fully intact.

She leans against the tree, breathes deeply, and enchants a dozen mothers with strollers to take their babies into their hands and walk in front of Patricia as she enters the playground. The women stand there cooing at their babies, oblivious to the confrontation, and blocking Patricia from passing.

"I can sense you, Doramae!" Patricia shouts over the crowd. "You won't outrun me!"

Patricia's aura is protected, and Doramae can't figure out who she is or the strength of her magical abilities, so she sends more mothers and children to fill the gap between them. A dog walker with five dogs on a leash joins the parade, and Doramae ducks out of sight behind a bush. She shields her aura from Patricia, but it's only a matter of time before Patricia counters her enchantment and clears the crowd.

"Where is she?" Jasmyn asks, breathless, as she arrives behind Patricia.

Patricia glares back at her. "I told you not to follow me!"

Doramae narrows her eyes to focus in on Jasmyn. Her lips curl into a snarl. "Finna's kin."

In two seconds, Doramae peeks into Jasmyn's unshielded aura, into her mind, her deepest sorrows, her greatest fears. Doramae lifts her right hand, narrows her eyes at Jasmyn, and whispers a spell.

A second later, Jasmyn sees Katarina's and Logan's slain bodies sprawled out in pools of blood at her feet. The scent of burning flesh and rotting corpses invade her senses. Her brother and sister beg Jasmyn for help, reaching their arms out, coughing and spitting up blood.

"No! Please, no," Jasmyn cries out.

In the dry, red desert of her hallucination, Jasmyn staggers back, falls to the ground, and hyperventilates, wailing at the images of her brother and sister crawling toward her.

When Patricia grabs Jasmyn's arms, Jasmyn doesn't see her coven sister—she sees her dead grandmother standing before her, with her flesh on fire and melting from her bones. She points her gory finger at Jasmyn and blames her for her siblings' deaths.

Jasmyn drops to her knees, takes hold of her grandmother's bony arms, and begs her for forgiveness, begs for the nightmare to end. "Stop! Please!" she shouts, crying and heaving. "I'm sorry! Please! I'm sorry!"

After several attempts, Patricia finally shields Jasmyn from Doramae's spell, and she catches her when she faints. She places Jasmyn gently onto the grass and runs to the edge of the park, then to the sidewalk along the street, and then to the next corner. She looks left and right, and curses when she no longer senses Doramae's aura.

17

COVEN SISTERS

Ever since Patricia learned of the broken blood spells, she's wondered if Jasmyn has enough training to stand up to powerful sorceresses like Loritida and Doramae. This encounter solidifies her doubt.

Patricia should have told Jasmyn of what she'd seen through the eyes of the filthy rat—a once-powerful sorceress who is now injured and weak enough for her to capture. She should have also explained why she told Jasmyn *not* to follow her.

But she didn't, and now Jasmyn is lying on a park bench, unconscious.

"What were you thinking?" Regina scolds over the phone.

Patricia gazes down at Jasmyn. A knot forms in her throat. "I thought I had her."

"I'm sure you could have taken her, but you can't leave Jasmyn in the dark like that."

"I told her to stay put. I didn't know she would follow me. And I didn't think she'd be that weak."

"She wasn't weak, she was unprepared—and unaware of Doramae's powers. You prepped her for the Foreman Clan before she went up against them. You did not prep her for this. She wasn't ready for mental spells. She wasn't ready—"

"I know!" Patricia shouts, pauses, and then sighs. "I know," she says in a calmer tone. "I didn't think it through. I'm sorry."

"Stop apologizing. I know you're angrier at yourself than I am." A few seconds pass in silence. "She's just sleeping, right?

No fever, shakes, talking in her sleep, nothing?"

"She's snoring a bit, but other than that, she looks like she's just taking a nap. Should I try to wake her?"

"No! You have no tact when it comes to these sorts of things. Damage done by mental spells has a way of healing itself through sleep, so don't interrupt it."

"Alright. I won't wake her," Patricia whispers harshly.

"I'm just now walking out of the terminal. Wow . . . Manchester Airport is packed. There is a ton of traffic in the pickup area. Lots of people. What kind of car is Gustavo driving?"

"A red SUV."

"I see him! Okay. Send me your location. Remember, don't wake Jasmyn. Let her sleep."

When Regina hangs up, Patricia stuffs her phone in her jacket, sighs, and rests Jasmyn's head on her lap. One by one, Patricia tucks loose strands of hair back from her face, imagining the horrific pictures Doramae must have fabricated to cause Jasmyn to react so frantically. She shakes her head.

This won't happen again. The minute you wake up, the second you're strong enough, I'll show you how to shield your aura so that no one can touch you.

A soft breeze blows against her cheeks, and Patricia feels a bit more confident than she did moments ago. Regina made a good point about Jasmyn's confrontation with the Foreman Clan—she was prepared for that battle. Today's battle came as a surprise. Jasmyn didn't know Doramae was there, or how much of a threat she posed. Patricia shakes her head, angry at herself for running off without an explanation.

I should have known better.

Since she can't wake her, Patricia whispers a few words, closes her eyes, and envisions a field of daisies and tall sunflowers stretching out to the horizon, with butterflies fluttering all around.

She imagines little Katarina running and Logan chasing her up the hill, giggles flowing in the air. The dream spell Regina taught her a week ago hasn't worked for her, but she tries and hopes it works now, if only to help Jasmyn heal from whatever hell Doramae put her through.

~ ~ ~

Since Doramae didn't know what she was walking into when she went to the address on Ryland's business card, the safest move was to use an inconspicuous rodent to take a first pass. And when those tiny black orbs showed her two women searching his chambers, she knew she'd made the right choice. Their conversation had revealed more than she expected.

Now, after driving for a half hour on the M61 in a stolen gray sedan, Doramae exits the highway and pulls into a gas station. She parks at the rear of the convenience store, away from the other cars, and shuts off the engine. The sound of the cars rolling on the highway overpass blow in with the spring breeze through the window. She recalls the conversation between Patricia and Jasmyn in Ryland's chambers.

Where have you been all this time, Loritida? Why did Finna banish you? Are you with Ryland? Do you know about this time-reversal spell?

Dozens more questions take form in Doramae's mind, and she shakes her head to dismiss them all. She recalls the last few times she saw Loritida, arguing in her defense, first asking that the coven grant her the immortal union, and then pleading for mercy after the Scyngar battle.

You were always on my side, cousin. You always supported me. Together, we can take revenge on Finna. Together, we can destroy Jasmyn.

Doramae rummages through the glove compartment in search of something sharp and finds a red army knife. She steps out of the car and heads to the bathroom around the back of the store.

Inside, she collects a pool of water in the sink and rolls up the sleeve on her left forearm to expose the swirl tattoo she and Loritida chose together when they were innocent teenagers, the best of friends, true coven sisters. Blood drips into the water when she digs the army knife into the black lines, and she recites a spell with her eyes closed—a spell that calls upon the mystical bond they created when they chose to imprint these tattoos onto their bodies. In two seconds, Doramae sees Loritida talking with Ryland. She narrows her eyes.

What are you up to, cousin?

18

A GIFT

When Loritida steps into the pub wearing the ivory wool coat Ryland chose for her, it's as if time has frozen. The five bearded men standing at the bar and the party of four sitting at a nearby table all put down their drinks and gawk at her beauty. Her jet-black hair glistens in the rays of sun shining in through the pub windows as she makes her way past the tables and chairs toward the dining room in the back. When her eyes finally meet Ryland's, he inhales deeply and smiles.

"Loritida, it has been a long, long time."

The scent of the oils and salts that Joseph put in her bath an hour before their meeting, as per Ryland's instructions, emanate from her skin. Ryland helps her with her coat, then takes her right hand and lifts it to his lips to plant a soft kiss.

"Too long," Loritida says with a smirk.

"I hope the Hotel Bergvik has provided you with adequate accommodations, and that Joseph has been treating you like a queen."

She smiles at Joseph. "He has been the most attentive of servants. I have not had a warm bath in centuries, and believe me, I needed one."

"It is the least I can do."

Ryland stretches out his hand to invite Loritida to sit down at a table set with a bottle of wine and two wine glasses. He gives Oregon a head-tilt, signifying the need for privacy.

"Joseph," Oregon says as he reaches for Joseph's arm,

"the local brew here is quite delicious. Will you join me for a pint?"

After a nod from Loritida, Joseph walks to the bar with Oregon, leaving them alone in the dining room. Ryland uncorks the bottle of merlot.

Loritida crosses one leg over the other and rests her hands on her knees. "Tell me, Ryland, how did you know where to find me?"

He fills each glass with wine. "I saw you in a vision," he says, avoiding Loritida's gaze.

"When?"

After a gulp, he decides that lying to her would be disastrous. "Around 1870. It was a long time ago—I can't remember the exact year."

She narrows her eyes. "And you're rescuing me now?"

Once the glasses are full, Ryland takes a seat and leans back in his chair. "I was serving the Foreman Clan when the visions came to me, and Caderyn always kept me close by his side. I couldn't break away." He sighs. "But he's dead, and now I'm free, so here I am. Besides"—he takes a sip from his glass and places it back on the table—"I could not free you from your prison. You would have only been vexed by my presence."

"I was alone."

"I understand it must have been difficult—"

"No, Ryland, you don't understand." She leans forward, and her voice deepens. "I was alone in ways you can't ever imagine."

He shifts in his seat and clears his throat. "My hands were tied. There was nothing I could do. Can you ever forgive me?"

Loritida rolls her eyes. "That depends." She finally picks up the glass of wine and takes a sip. She holds the glass close to her lips as she swallows, hiding any signs of discomfort as the liquid burns the sores lining her throat. With a graceful stretch, she places the glass down and smirks. "I sense that you have a plan of some sort. A scheme."

He leans back and smiles.

"I knew it."

"There's so much to explain that I don't know where to start."

"My love." Loritida gazes deeply into Ryland's eyes and speaks in a silky voice. "Why don't you just tell me what you need from me, and if I see that it's worth my while, I will help you. It's the least I could do for you for rescuing me from that cave." She smiles softly, bats her eyelashes, and leans back in her chair. "And if you lie to me, or if I sense that you're lying to me, I will pull your flesh from your bones and feed you to the dogs."

He sighs and lowers his gaze to his hands. Dealing with complicated sorceresses was never something Ryland was good at, and Loritida was a whirlwind of highs and lows. Hate and love, anger and glee, lust and revenge always colliding with one another—despite the risks, he loves Loritida's unpredictable nature.

He decides to start from the beginning. "Do you know why you are free from Finna's blood spell?"

She narrows her eyes. "Jasmyn, Finna's kin, released me."

Ryland raises his eyebrows in surprise. "You know about Jasmyn?"

"I learned a thing or two from this." She lifts her arm to show Ryland her bracelet. "Finna gave it to me as a gift."

"And you kept it all this time?"

She smiles as she pulls the bracelet around her wrist. "I kept it to remind me of the person who put me in that prison. I've untied and retied it so many times, watching her live freely throughout the centuries. And then I watched her daughter, Agatha . . ."

Loritida unfolds her legs, adjusts herself in her seat, and crosses them again.

Ryland studies Loritida silently as she formulates her thoughts.

"When I was first imprisoned, I promised myself that if I ever escaped, I would find Finna or her kin and kill them. But after so much time has passed," she inhales deeply and closes her eyes for a second before opening them, "I find myself conflicted. After being alone for so long, the thought of rejoining the coven is very tempting. After all, Jasmyn freed me from the blood spell. She must want me back."

"Well, you're wrong about Jasmyn. She didn't release you. Your blood spell was broken."

Ryland takes a sip of his wine and watches cautiously as Loritida's high, arched eyebrows flatten. Her lips press into a tight line, and her soft expression of hope transforms into distrust and suspicion.

"She . . . didn't . . . release me?"

"No."

She scans him from the top of his head down to his fancy shoes.

He has the urge to move, but he holds still against her glare.

"Finna has kin. How can her spell be broken?"

"Let's just call it serendipity." He sets down his glass of wine. "In any case, soon after Agatha died, your blood spell was broken, and I had a vision of you waking from your sleep, and—"

"You saw me?" She looks away.

"Yes." He takes her hand. "I know what you truly look like. It doesn't matter to me."

Loritida snatches her hand back, avoiding his gaze.

"And I know that it's only a matter of time before you are

fully restored to your former self, to the beautiful, powerful woman that I—"

In a breath faster than his own, amid a rustle of chairs and crashing of tables, Ryland finds himself pinned against the wall with Loritida's hand at his throat. His feet dangle in the air.

"Don't believe for one second that you can manipulate me with your flattery."

"I . . . don't . . ."

Ryland desperately searches the room for Oregon and Joseph, but he can't see past a dividing wall. He and Loritida are out of view of anyone else in the pub. Combine that with the noise of the big-screen televisions broadcasting a local football game and the patrons cheering for their home team, she is free to do what she will without any interference.

When he looks back at her, his eyes widen with horror as the lovely, desirable woman who greeted him earlier transforms into a wretched troll with pus-filled cheeks and a spotted, balding scalp.

She releases her grip on his throat and steps back and away. Ryland tumbles to the ground as she whispers a spell over and over so that her porcelain skin and silky black hair return. He scrambles to his feet and stands with his back against the wall, breathing heavily.

"Do not play with me, Ryland," she says with a rasp. She clears her throat, closes her eyes, whispers another spell, and then continues in the same sultry voice as before. "Get to the point. Why have you brought me here?"

Ryland staggers away from the wall, straightening his suit jacket and tie, and then places his right hand over his heart. "I came bearing gifts." He gestures toward the table and picks up two fallen chairs. Once both chairs are upright, he offers one to Loritida.

With slow, deliberate movements, she sits back in the chair and crosses her legs. Her eyes are still narrowed at him.

"Gifts?" she asks in a sour tone. A slight curl in Loritida's lips puts Ryland at ease.

He drags the rolling suitcase from the corner of the dining room, lays it flat on the ground, and opens it. He pulls out the dragon egg and hands it to her. "Consider this as a token of my affection, or rather, my intentions."

She gasps, and her crystal-blue eyes widen. "Where did you get this?"

"It's yours."

"It's . . . it's . . . magnificent." She smiles grandly.

As Loritida's smile mesmerizes him, he wonders if her lips feel and taste the same as when he last kissed her so long ago. Then he recalls the wretch living under the beautiful facade and decides to wait a little longer to find out.

With careful twists and turns, Loritida inspects every inch of the iridescent scales covering the dragon egg. Arrays of pink and blue shimmer from the gunmetal base as she lifts it into the lamplight. She lowers it back down to eye level and places it on her lap.

"This is impressive."

"I've had that dragon egg for a long time, and not once did I mention it to Caderyn."

"Why not?"

He leans in closer, gazes deep into her eyes, and softens his voice. "I was saving it for the right moment."

"And this is the right moment because . . . ?" She raises her eyebrows and smirks.

After a long inhale, Ryland lowers his gaze for two seconds and then lifts it to meet Loritida's eager stare. "Finna had the ability to travel back to the past within her own lifetime. She executed this time-reversal magic once and changed the course of her coven's history. Agatha inherited that magic, and now Jasmyn has it."

"You've seen Finna use this magic?" she asks, her eyebrows furrowed.

"Yes. I saw her do it, through my visions."

"Very well. What does any of that have to do with me?"

Rylan leans back in his seat. "Jasmyn's brother and sister have recently passed away. I believe Jasmyn will use this magic to go back in time to prevent their deaths. Probably back a few weeks ago before Agatha passed away. Which means . . . your blood spell will be intact."

Loritida gasps. "No. I'll be trapped in that cave again."

"And remain there until Agatha or Jasmyn chooses to release you."

"Which will never happen." Her throat goes dry. "All those nights that seemed to never end . . . the snowstorms . . . the loneliness . . . the bugs . . ." She trails off, hyperventilating.

Ryland places a hand on her arm. "Fortunately, as serendipity would have it, Jasmyn didn't inherit Agatha's memories, so she doesn't know how to execute the spell."

Loritida regains her composure. She gazes up at him with fear in her eyes.

He continues, "She doesn't know how to execute the spell, but I do. I've seen Agatha do it. I know exactly what needs to be done."

As if a switch was flipped, Loritida's fright transforms into a confident smirk. She leans back in her chair, crosses her legs suggestively, and narrows her eyes at Ryland. "What, exactly, is your plan?"

Ryland nods. "It was Kean's plan, actually. He was going to consume Jasmyn's heart to gain her powers and perform the time-reversal spell himself to change the clan's history. He came really close."

"What stopped him?"

"Jasmyn has a dragon. It killed Kean."

Loritida raises her eyebrows. "She has a dragon?"

"Yes." He places his hand on the egg. "And now, so do you."

She squints at him. "I trust you know how to birth dragon eggs."

"Me, personally? No." He reaches into his bag, pulls out the Book of Sol, and sets it softly on the table. "But you can find the spell here."

She gasps. "You still have it!"

"Of course. When a powerful sorceress such as yourself grants me a book of spells . . . well . . . let's just say it's one of my most valuable possessions."

For the first time since she arrived, Loritida weakens her guard and gazes upon Ryland with that old fondness, letting him in, trusting him completely as she once did.

Ryland is unable to contain his smile. "I told you I bear gifts."

"You certainly do, Ryland. You certainly do."

19

TREASURES

As Jasmyn lies unconscious on a park bench under a hundred-year-old oak, Regina waves a candle over her head and whispers a spell into her ear. Once Regina completes the spell, Jasmyn opens her eyes, blinks several times, and sluggishly sits up.

The afternoon sun shines brighter than normal on her sensitive eyes, and she rubs her eyelids with her fingers. A loud rustle of leaves echoes in her ears as squirrels scramble through the branches of the oak tree. The scent of lavender invades her nostrils.

"How do you feel?" Regina asks.

Jasmyn takes a few deep breaths to calm her senses. "Fine." Through squinted eyes, she glances at her Uncle Gustavo, who is kneeling in front of her. She blocks the blaring sunlight with her hand and peers up at Regina and Patricia. "What happened?"

"What's the last thing you remember?" Patricia asks.

As the fluorescent bushes fade to their normal green with each blink, Jasmyn recalls the last moments before everything went blank. "I was running after you, across the street to this playground. It was full of people, lots of dogs and kids. There were a ton of moms holding babies in their arms, and . . ."

The rocks on the paved floor seem to tremble when Jasmyn glances at them. They wobble as if dancing in circles around her feet, breaking into pieces. She closes her eyes for two seconds, then opens them and refocuses her vision. The rocks lie still, unbroken.

Regina's floral dress draws her attention, the colorful roses spinning and the petals on the yellow daisies fluttering. She narrows her eyes at the design, blinks a few more times, and the flowers stop moving. The smell of lavender fades, and the squirrel no longer runs amok in the branches over her head.

She glances back up at Patricia. "That's it. I don't remember anything else."

"Memory loss may be a good thing," Regina says. "Whatever Doramae put in your head made you go crazy. It's better you don't remember it."

"I went crazy?" Jasmyn turns to Patricia.

Patricia nods. "It was scary. You cried out Kat and Logan's names. You screamed like I've never heard you scream before."

"It's a good thing you shielded Jasmyn as soon as you did." Regina looks up at Patricia. "These hallucination spells can be disastrous. Doramae could have made Jasmyn stab herself, or run in front of a bus, or jump off a bridge. And by the way you describe Jasmyn's reaction, it seems like Doramae was heading in that direction."

The thought of Jasmyn getting hit by a bus makes Patricia shiver. She shakes her head and glances toward Gustavo but doesn't look directly into his eyes. She can't face him right now.

"Looks like the damage is superficial," Regina says, blowing out her candle. "She'll be fine with a little rest."

Gustavo reaches out for her arm. "Try standing up."

When Jasmyn rises to her feet, her head spins and her knees wobble. She grabs her uncle's arm and takes two long, deep breaths. The dizziness dissipates before she makes her way to the car.

"I'm really sorry, Gustavo," Patricia says, walking alongside them, staring at the ground. "She'll be more prepared the next time we encounter Doramae."

"I know you're sorry, so please stop apologizing," Gustavo says sharply. He doesn't look at Patricia. "Let's just get her to the car. It's a long ride to Newcastle."

"Don't worry, Jasmyn," Regina says, zipping up her satchel full of crystals, candles, herbs, and other items stowed in small plastic bags. She shoulders the strap and catches up to them. "I'll undo anything Doramae did by the time we get to Newcastle. You'll be good as new."

The four sit quietly in the truck as Gustavo drives onto the highway and picks up speed. No one has said a word since they left the park. From the back, Jasmyn notices the frown on her uncle's face and sees Patricia slumping toward the door in the front passenger seat. She can sense the tension between the two of them.

Jasmyn nudges Regina and tilts her head toward Gustavo and Patricia.

Regina leans toward her and whispers, "He's angry at Patricia for what Doramae did to you, and she feels guilty for letting it happen."

"But it wasn't her fault," Jasmyn whispers back.

"Give them a little time to calm down."

After a few more minutes of silence, Jasmyn says, "You know, right before I woke up in the park, I was dreaming of running in a field of daisies and sunflowers with Logan and Kat. It was weird. We're usually on a beach or a mountain. I don't really dream with flowers. There were daisies everywhere."

Patricia gasps. She spins in her seat and looks at Regina, wide-eyed. "That was me! I used your dream spell to force those images into Jasmyn's head while she was sleeping on my lap. It finally worked!"

Regina smiles. "You're opening up to new ways of conducting magic." She raises her eyebrows at Jasmyn. "See . . . you *can* teach an old dog new tricks."

"Speaking of new tricks." Patricia turns back to the road. "Both of you need to learn to shield your auras. Hide them from anyone who can sense magic."

"How do you hide your aura?" Jasmyn asks.

Regina tapped the window with her knuckles and looks out the window. "Patricia's the master at hiding and cloaking and that sort of thing. She hid from me so well I couldn't find her for decades, and I can locate just about anyone with the right token."

"Why did she hide from you?"

Patricia turns her head slightly. "I had issues back then. What was it . . . 1950s . . . 1960s? I didn't want anyone to find me." Her phone rings. She pulls it out of her pocket. "I have to take this."

Regina leans close to Jasmyn and speaks quietly. "It had something to do with Agatha starting a family. Agatha wanted us to stay away. I think Patricia felt rejected, abandoned. She shut us both out. In any case, it's a good skill to have."

She places a hand on her chest and continues, "I'm more of an open book, which is why, I believe, I can communicate with nature better than she can. It comes naturally to me. But, then again, I'm okay with elemental spells, where Patricia is a master. I mean, you've seen Patricia fight."

"Oh, yeah." Jasmyn's eyes widen.

"She can move mountains and make the earth shake, and she can use elemental spells for a long time. I collapse after a few minutes; she can go on for hours. And she has an amazing shielding ability—remember how she blocked that fire from Baronyx?"

"I remember."

"One hit from that dragon, and I was out for a week!"

Jasmyn smirks as she recalls Regina limping in the hospital.

"She fights dragons, fights the Foreman Clan, and hasn't so much as a cut or a bruise. But healing and communicating with nature"—Regina points her thumbs at herself—"I'm the master at that. Now, lean back and let me do my thing."

Jasmyn sinks back in her seat, rests her hands on her stomach, and closes her eyes. "Did you ever see Nana?" She opens her eyes to make sure Regina heard her question.

"Oh, no." Regina purses her lips. "I wrote to her and called her every now and then, but I stayed away. It was her wish that her family didn't know about us or her past. She wanted a normal life for them."

Jasmyn sighs.

With her fingers interlocked, Regina twists her hands until her palms face forward, then stretches her arms out in front of her. "Your grandmother had so much love for you. The last few times I spoke to her over the phone, all she did was gush about you, Logan, and Katarina. She said you were her treasures."

The word *treasure* conjures up images of the one trinket Jasmyn treasured the most, her grandmother's dragon pendant. It was Agatha's most cherished relic. Many long, lazy afternoons were spent playing dress-up with her grandmother—fancy hats, frilly scarves, exquisite necklaces, and colorful gems from all over the world were at their disposal. Once Jasmyn finished her wild outfit, Agatha would top the ensemble by placing the dragon pendant around her neck.

Jasmyn had expressed her fondness for the charm so many times that Agatha promised it would be hers.

It's been years since Jasmyn's worn it. She can't recall the last time she held it in her hands, or even where it is at this very

112

moment—probably stuffed inside one of the containers holding Nana's things back home. The one thing she *can* recall is how it hung around Katarina's neck the day after their grandmother passed away, and how it made her rage with jealousy.

Jasmyn shivers, frowning with shame as the memory pierces her heart. She'd give anything to have her baby sister prancing around wearing her grandmother's jewelry right now, as she used to when she was a little girl. A single tear streams down her cheek. She wipes her face dry before Regina notices.

"Now, close your eyes," Regina says. "We've got a few hours before we reach Newcastle, so rest easy."

After a long inhale, Jasmyn complies. She senses Regina's aura pressing against her body, penetrating her muscles with its rejuvenating vibrations. As the conversation in the car continues, her muscles melt against the seat.

Patricia ends her call. "That was Evan. He called to see if we have any hiking equipment and cold gear. He's ready and waiting for us."

"You told him we have nothing, right?" Gustavo asks in a calmer tone.

"Yeah. He's getting us all the equipment we need."

"Who's Evan?" Regina asks.

"Evan Morrison is from my platoon," Gustavo says. "He lives in Newcastle, owns an outdoor-gear store, and rents yachts. He's taking us to the Isle of Enid."

"Oooh," Regina says. "Evan Morrison has a tall, strong, handsome ring to it. Like a lumberjack."

Jasmyn snorts and giggles.

"Shush!" Regina scolds her. "Think about someplace far away, like… Hawaii."

Regina places her hand on Jasmyn's forehead. A soft hum of a tropical melody fills her ears, and she can almost hear waves crashing along a shore.

"Breath deep," Regina whispers. "Relax, and just watch the sun setting behind the palm trees. Someone playing the ukulele. Waves crashing. Seagulls chirping far away."

"I hate seagulls," Jasmyn mumbles.

"Shh!"

After a few minutes, Jasmyn finds herself walking barefoot on a beach at noon, the clear blue ocean on her left and a row of palm trees on her right. A warm breeze brushes against her skin as she strolls along the white sand. She discovers an unusual connection with the sand, water, and air in her dream environment.

She looks at her palms and raises her arms, and the ocean water rises with her. It holds its position in the sky until she forces it to crash down onto the beach in perfect waves. She juts out her fingers, picks up gallons of sand, and forms a tornado that spins straight up. When she swings her arms out to the side, the sand tornado disperses as if it were never there.

While Regina performs her healing spells, Jasmyn falls deeper and deeper into an unconscious state. In her dream, she is invigorated and energized. Regina's magic is working—she is so much stronger than when she awoke in the park. So, instead of resting and dreaming peacefully as Regina suggested, Jasmyn practices executing elemental spells. She picks up a giant rock and tosses it far into the ocean, causing a spout to spray up toward the sky. Jasmyn's chest swells, and she nods at having complete control of the elements—the way Patricia always seems to.

The next time we meet, Doramae, I won't be so easy to dominate.

20

REMEMBERING

It doesn't take too much magic to make the airline attendant in Manchester Airport book Doramae on the next flight to Iceland.

Although all flights are full, the young man doesn't hesitate to cancel a passenger and reassign the seat. When Doramae finally arrives in Akureyri Airport a few hours later, she singles out a black-suited man holding a sign that reads, *Jon Grímsson*, and asks if he could be her personal driver for the day. The driver, like the young airline attendant, doesn't have a chance against her charm, and leads her to his Mercedes-Benz SUV.

When the driver rolls out of the airport, Doramae gives him a general direction, toward Loritida's aura, pointing out of the car at a distant hill. As the driver gets closer to her destination, he goes off-road onto a rocky path that loops up and around the hill. He apologizes to Doramae for the choppy ride.

"Stop right here," Doramae says just before they reach the summit.

"I can take you all the way to the top, ma'am."

"No. Right here is fine. You will return to the airport and forget you ever saw me. Is that understood?"

"Yes, ma'am."

The car drives back down the road, the driver already forgetting Doramae's face.

Doramae's legs are now fully recovered, her body back to its full strength, so she treks up the last portion of the hill, cloaking her aura so that no one detects her presence.

When she reaches the top, she sees a truck parked at the end of the gravel road. An old man sleeps in the driver's seat, his arm hanging out the open window. Doramae tiptoes up to the truck and lightly taps the back of the old man's hand.

Ryland's only friend and confidant. You might be useful to me.

She makes her way across the hilltop and stops when she hears the crackle of fire mingling with voices on the other side of a boulder. Loritida's familiar voice causes the hairs on Doramae's back to straighten, and she is overcome with melancholy. She closes her eyes, takes a long breath, and peeks past the large rock.

Loritida is in full view, and Ryland stands at her side.

"Stop right there, Joseph," Loritida shouts. "Now, turn around and face me."

Stretching her neck out, Doramae sees a man holding a large egg. She watches them silently.

With her hands open wide and her stare firmly set on her target, Loritida bellows out the enchanted words to merge Joseph with the dragon egg, triggering the dragon's birth. Joseph is engulfed in a glowing haze for a few seconds before Loritida screams with frustration and drops to her knees. The glow disappears, and Joseph stumbles, falling onto his back.

Joseph stands up, gives his body a quick inspection, and sighs with relief.

After five failed attempts, Loritida shouts even louder. She storms away from the fire, trips, and falls to her knees.

Ryland carefully sets the Book of Sol flat on the ground and then lifts Loritida by the arm. "You are not yet strong enough for this kind of magic. Why don't you rest? We can try again in an hour."

"No!" Once she reaches her feet, she yanks her arm out of

Ryland's hold. She faces him squarely. "I don't want to waste more time. I've waited long enough to get my revenge on Finna. I don't want to wait any longer."

"Look at your hands."

Loritida raises her hands and splays out her fingers, then gasps at the warts and rotting flesh. She steps away from Ryland, crosses her arms, and stuffs her hands in her armpits.

"Your cover-up spell is fading as you weaken," he says. "This is taking a toll on you. If you weaken yourself too much, it will only take longer to birth the dragon." He places his hand on her back. "You're not yet fully recovered. Let us rest for a few hours and try again."

Loritida groans. "Fine."

"Joseph!" Ryland calls out. "Bring the egg here and get the truck!"

Joseph runs over to Ryland and Loritida and carefully places the dragon egg at Loritida's feet. Then he dashes over to the other side of the hill, where their truck is parked.

With a gentle nudge, Ryland turns Loritida around to face him. He caresses her cheek with the back of his hand. "You'll have more strength if you just rest for a bit."

Loritida grunts. "I'm not tired. I can still—"

"Don't push yourself. You don't want to mess this up. If you rest, you will rejuvenate, your muscles will toughen up, your powers will strengthen, and maybe then you'll be able to execute the spell. Okay?"

Loritida nods and rests her head on Ryland's chest.

Doramae rolls her eyes as Ryland easily manipulates her cousin. She can't decide what angers her more, Loritida's weakness or Ryland's impertinence. She spits to the side and glares at them with disdain.

How could you have let yourself become this vulnerable,

Loritida? You were the leader of our coven. You led us to victory in multiple wars. And now . . . this is what you have become? You allow Ryland, an old seer, to control you? How could you let this happen?

Doramae shakes her head.

I've seen enough.

After removing her magical cloak, Doramae appears right next to the Book of Sol. With a forceful tug, she lifts the ancient book into her arms and opens it to the bookmarked page. She reviews the old writing, nods, and shuts the book.

Startled by the *thud* of the book slamming, Ryland and Loritida whirl around.

"Doramae!" Ryland says nervously. He glances at the Book of Sol in her arms, then meets her gaze. "What . . . how?"

"You seem surprised, Ryland. As an elder and seer, I would have thought you'd see me coming."

Stunned, Ryland stands with his mouth open, staring at Doramae as she walks toward Loritida. As she gets closer to Loritida, Ryland takes a step away.

"Do you remember me, cousin?" Doramae asks.

"Cousin?" Loritida replies, glancing at Ryland.

She stops two feet in front of Loritida and rolls up the sleeve of her right forearm to display her swirl tattoo. "Do you remember when we got this?"

Loritida lifts her own sleeve and sees the same marking. "Yes. It's coming back to me." She looks up at Doramae. "Why is that? Why is my memory of you so . . . distorted?"

Doramae takes a deep breath. "The coven sentenced me to a Forgotten Existence."

A landslide of memories rushes over Loritida. Their childhood as little girls, unaware of the complexities of the world, as teenagers experimenting with their new powers, as adults exercising and testing the limits of their abilities—it all crystallizes.

"Doramae!" She smiles, and her eyes widen.

A second later, she remembers the battle with the Scyngars, the trial, and Finna's sentence. Her smile transforms into a stiff frown, and her eyebrows wrinkle with sadness. A loud gulp escapes her, and her bottom lip trembles.

"Oh, Doramae, I'm so sorry."

Loritida runs to her cousin and embraces her tightly, whispering praises of gratitude to the old gods. She pulls away and puts her hands on Doramae's cheeks. "Please forgive me, cousin. I never wanted to sentence you to a Forgotten Existence. The coven wanted to kill you, and this was the only compromise." She embraces her again. "It was the only way to keep you alive. It was the only way the coven would let you live."

Doramae returns Loritida's embrace, but not with as much sincerity. "I forgive you, cousin. You did what you could."

Doramae glares sideways at Ryland. She can read his fears, and she chuckles devilishly. "So, Ryland, the Foreman Clan is gone, and you no longer have your visions. What use is an old seer who sees nothing?"

"I helped save Loritida," he says in a shaky voice. He clears his throat. "I rescued her from that cave. I—"

Doramae turns her back to Ryland, facing Loritida. She lifts her tattooed arm. "Remember our oath?"

Loritida looks at her forearm and remembers the spell they shared, intermingling the tattoo ink with each other's blood as teenage girls learning their mothers' magic. She whispers, "I remember every word."

For a moment, Doramae gazes upon her cousin with fondness, recalling how young and innocent they were when they inked their tattoos and enchanted them with the spell. They formed a mystical bond stronger than that of natural sisters, one that could only be broken by death.

But when Loritida looks back at Ryland, Doramae's affection is replaced by disappointment. At that moment, she remembers how easily persuadable Loritida was as coven leader, manipulated by the older sisters, by anyone who would show her praise. She never managed the pressures of leadership gracefully; she was never able to move the coven the way Finna could.

Nevertheless, she needs Loritida if she is to confront the coven. Jasmyn may be weak, but Patricia has proven herself a formidable opponent. She takes a deep breath and hides her disdain, for now.

Doramae interlocks her arm with Loritida's and walks away from Ryland. Arm in arm, they stroll around the firepit. Ryland follows behind, listening intently.

"I know all about your plan to consume Jasmyn's heart and use the time-reversal spell," Doramae says.

Loritida stops walking and turns to face her cousin. "You do?"

"I saw your interaction with Ryland in the waters."

Loritida nods. They resume their stroll.

"Tell me, cousin, what has happened to you?" Doramae asks gently. "Why are you so physically strained? Why do you feel you need the help of this blind seer?"

Staring at the ground, her head hanging low, Loritida replies in a defeated tone, "A long time ago ... Finna and the coven rebelled against me." Loritida meets Doramae's stare. "They banished me."

Of course. Doramae rolls her eyes. "Go on."

"Finna became the coven leader after," Ryland says from a few feet behind them. "Then her daughter, Agatha, inherited leadership, and now—"

In a blink, Doramae lifts Ryland off his feet, her hand around his throat. "If you say one more word, I will squeeze your neck until your eyes pop out of their sockets."

Loritida wraps her fingers around Doramae's wrist. "Please, don't. Ryland is helping me."

"You no longer need his help."

"He knows how to execute the time-reversal spell."

He kicks wildly.

Doramae only tightens her grip. "Once you consume Jasmyn's heart, you will have knowledge of the time-reversal spell as well."

"No . . . she . . . won't," Ryland manages.

"Please, Doramae. Let him go."

The fact that Loritida, a powerful sorceress many centuries old, is pleading for the life of an elder, a so-called seer who can't see anything, makes Doramae cringe.

What hold does this useless seer have on you? Have you no shame?

With the little strength she has left, Loritida slams both her arms against Doramae's shoulders. Doramae releases her grip, and Ryland collapses sideways to the ground like a rag doll. He scrambles to his knees, gasping for air.

Doramae takes two steps back and glares at Loritida. "You would attack me? For *him*?"

"Jasmyn doesn't have Finna's memories!" Loritida shouts, standing over Ryland, her arms up in defense. "She doesn't have Agatha's knowledge or history, so she doesn't know how to execute the spell."

After a few more coughs, Ryland rises and dusts himself off. "I know exactly what needs to be done." He clears his throat. "I saw it in my visions."

Doramae rolls her eyes at Loritida. "And you can't get this

knowledge from him?"

"You know seers are not susceptible to our magic."

Doramae lifts her fist. "You don't need magic to get information out of him."

Ryland huffs and smirks. "I have been tortured and mangled by sorcerers far greater than you. I have nothing to gain by giving you the time-reversal spell, and everything to lose if I do." He gazes at Loritida. "I will share it with Loritida and no one else."

"Ryland is on our side. He has centuries of knowledge at our disposal. He's useful to us." Loritida swallows hard and looks deeper into Doramae's eyes. "Please, Doramae. If you kill him, we won't know anything about the spell."

Unconvinced, Doramae glares at them in turn.

As the northern sun descends toward the horizon and the cool breeze warns of the evening chill, Loritida leans close to Doramae. "If you help me, I'll go back in time far enough to kill Finna and all the other coven sisters who denied you and Moran the immortal union—I'll go back to a time before anyone even knew about your affair."

Doramae gasps. Her lips part as Moran's smile flashes in her mind. She blinks back sudden tears.

Loritida straightens, inhales deeply, and sneers. "And I will make sure that no one—and I mean no one—will imprison us ever again. I swear to it."

21

DEFENSES

While Regina and Jasmyn sleep in the back seat, Patricia thinks of Doramae, Loritida, and the coven. Memories of Doramae, or rather, her mother's memories, trickle in slowly, but there is nothing solid she can use to see Doramae's full capabilities.

You've used dark magic, she thinks. *You led an invasion of the Isle of Enid. You have strong mental-manipulation skills. However, you didn't stand and fight me. You ran. You attacked Jasmyn because she was weaker than me. Weaker than you. Do you not have any elemental skills? Are your fighting skills weak? And where is Loritida in all of this?*

"We're here," Gustavo says as he drives past the marina's welcome sign, breaking Patricia's reverie. He parks in a lot and shuts off the engine.

"Is that Evan?" Patricia asks.

A bald man with a goatee walks up to the truck, grinning.

"Yeah," Gustavo says, smiling grandly. "That's him, alright."

She studies him, taking in his all-black attire: tactical military pants, boots, and a T-shirt. *Regina will be all over this one.*

Gustavo and Patricia both climb out of the truck to greet Evan. With arms open wide, Gustavo gives the newcomer a bear hug. They pound each other's backs, their laughter so loud it wakes Regina and Jasmyn from their deep sleep.

"Ooh . . . is that our much-anticipated Evan Morrison?" Regina runs her hands through her hair and straightens her dress, then digs in her bag and pulls out a mirror.

With a chuckle, Jasmyn opens the door and steps outside to stretch her arms, legs, and back. As she twists from side to side, Gustavo walks over with Evan.

"Evan, this is my niece, Jasmyn," Gustavo says, a hint of pride in his tone. "Jaz, Evan Morrison was in my platoon in Afghanistan. He's the captain of the ship we're sailing on."

"Good to meet you, Jasmyn," says Evan. "I've heard so much about you."

Evan's wide smile is infectious, and Jasmyn can't help but smile back at him. She shakes his hand. His deep blue aura catches her attention—the same strong, noble aura her uncle has.

Regina gets out of the car on Jasmyn's side and stretches her hand out toward Evan. "I'm Regina Meyer, at your service," she says with a coy smirk.

Evan takes her hand and gazes into her eyes. "It's very nice to meet you, Regina."

Gustavo clears his throat. "Regina is a sorceress, just like Patricia."

"Right. A sorceress . . ." Evan turns away from Regina's sultry gaze and faces Gustavo. "My crew is at a pub. Are you all hungry?"

Everyone nods.

"Great. Follow me." Evan heads toward a line of small stores along the marina. "It'll give us a bit of time to go over some things with the crew."

"You guys go ahead," Patricia calls, walking toward the water. "Jasmyn and I will be on the pier."

"Okay." Regina smooths her skirt and catches up with Evan and Gustavo. "We'll see you later."

When Patricia and Jasmyn reach the end of the empty pier, Patricia gazes left and right across the entire breadth of the sea. A biting breeze blows her hair away from her face.

"I forget how cold it gets this far north in springtime." Patricia shivers and zips up her black leather jacket. "It's a good thing Evan has cold gear for us. Hiking boots, too, for when we reach the island."

"What are we doing here?" Jasmyn asks.

"We're going to practice blocking mental-manipulation spells."

Patricia hears footsteps and spots an elderly couple meandering down the pier. The old man pulls the hood of the lady's beige jacket over her white hair, stuffing the loose strands into the hood. Once her head is covered, he lifts his own hood and buttons up the top of his parka before they both sit on a bench.

"Perfect," Patricia says. "You can practice your mental spells on them."

"What? No." Jasmyn furrows her eyebrows. "I don't want to do to them what Doramae did to me."

Patricia chuckles. "Relax. You're not that strong yet. Start with something small, like making them sit, stand, or walk. I can't show you how to block manipulation magic until you know what it is you are blocking."

"What about shielding my aura? Will that block manipulation magic?"

"That's different. You shield your aura so other sorcerers can't learn anything about you. They can detect your presence, but nothing more. You can't be an open book like Regina. Look what Doramae did when she read your aura and learned of Kat's and Logan's deaths. She used it against you. She implanted visions in your head that made you go crazy."

Jasmyn feels a sense of relief that she doesn't remember the hallucinations.

"It's a very powerful ability," Patricia continues. "It's not only hallucinations. The mind controls the body. You can break bones, twist muscles, knock people off their feet with mental manipulations. You must learn to block it."

A burst of laughter from the old couple draws their attention.

Patricia points her chin at them. "Now, make that couple stand."

Jasmyn narrows her eyes at her targets and repeats a command in her head over and over.

Nothing happens. She takes a deep breath, shakes out her arms, stretches her neck side to side, and tries again.

"You're trying too hard. I can actually see your body tense up. This is a mental spell. You only need to use this muscle." Patricia points at her head. "Relax. Close your eyes. Feel the wind against your body. Whisper the command as you breathe."

Jasmyn nods and shuts her eyes.

"You can sense their presence, right?" Patricia whispers, her mouth near Jasmyn's ear. "Feel their presence in your hands. First, picture one of them in your mind, then the other, and envision them doing exactly what you want."

A soft breeze passes over the marina. Jasmyn lifts her head, eyes still closed, and allows the wind to caress her face. She senses the old couple's aura, sighing as she feels their warm love for each other, their jittery worries about their children and grandchildren, and their crushing fears for each other's health.

After a few seconds, Jasmyn sees, in her mind, the old woman standing and strolling to the other side of the pier and back. Soon, she sees the husband do the same thing. In her vision, the sunset blazes orange and red hues from behind the line of stores along the marina. It draws her attention, and she sighs as the colorful light.

"Open your eyes," Patricia whispers.

126

When she does, Jasmyn watches the couple march to one end of the pier and back, just as she's envisioned. Their faces are serene, expressionless, as if hypnotized.

Jasmyn whispers, "Return to what you were doing before," and they both sit back down and continue their conversation as if nothing happened.

"That was pretty good. See—no one was hurt," Patricia says with a smirk.

Jasmyn smiles.

"Okay, now do the same thing, and make them *see* something that's not there."

"Like what?"

"I don't know." Patricia raises her shoulders as she looks around. "Like a bird or a frog or a duck."

Jasmyn nods, closes her eyes, and peeks into the old lady's aura once more. She learns of their recently deceased pet, so she envisions the same little black Scottish terrier, as a puppy, bouncing in front of them, nipping at their hands playfully, licking their fingers.

When she opens her eyes, she sees the couple stroking an invisible dog and laughing.

The old lady says, "Oh, Alfred, he looks exactly like Mr. Jingles!"

"Mr. Jingles?" Patricia chuckles.

"It was their fifteen-year-old dog. It died last year." Jasmyn shrugs. "I wanted to see if I could conjure up an image that meant something to them."

After a few minutes, Jasmyn makes the puppy run away toward land, and the couple watches it until it disappears in the distance.

Patricia purses her lips and nods proudly. "Very good. So, now you have to learn to block what you just did." She faces

Jasmyn again. "What would you do if I physically attacked you right now?"

Jasmyn crosses her arms. "I'd shield myself from your attack."

"Right. Now you must do the mental equivalent of blocking an attack. Mental manipulation is making someone do or see something without them realizing you are controlling what they're doing or seeing."

Patricia stares into Jasmyn's eyes, and Jasmyn begins hopping on one foot.

Thirty seconds pass before Jasmyn catches wind of Patricia's manipulation. She smiles the instant she feels the magic, and another minute passes while she figures out how to free herself from Patricia's hold.

"That was a good start." Patricia nods. "The more we practice, the quicker you'll get at blocking manipulations of what you *do*. Now, try to block this."

When Jasmyn sees mice and birds nipping at her arms and legs, she squeals and dodges them.

"They're an illusion," Patricia says calmly.

Jasmyn flails at the creatures, trying to decipher what is real and what isn't.

"Yes!" she shouts the moment she identifies the sensation. Although it takes a bit longer, Jasmyn eventually learns how to block Patricia's hallucinations.

"Wow. They seemed so real!" Jasmyn says in awe.

"Hallucinations are harder to identify."

Jasmyn nods, and her eyes light up with an idea. "You said Doramae planted images of my brother and sister in my head—made me see things that made me scream, that drove me crazy." She glances at the wooden panels beneath her feet. "Can you make me see those types of images?"

Patricia grimaces. "Why?"

"So I can practice warding them off. Can you do that for me?"

"I'm not sure I can . . ." Patricia frowns, shaking her head.

"You heard Regina," Jasmyn says. "If you didn't stop Doramae's attack, she could have made me walk out in front of a moving bus. I need to defend myself against anything Doramae might throw at me."

Patricia stares at her, sadness in her eyes. "Those images are painful when they appear out of nowhere, subconsciously. You want me to deliberately visualize them?"

"I need to do this, Patricia." Jasmyn sighs. "You can't protect me forever. I must learn to protect myself. Only you can help me get stronger."

A sense of pride at Jasmyn's independent attitude overcomes her. It's immediately drowned out by the knowledge that she's about to cause her immense heartache with these hallucinations. She swallows hard and nods forlornly. "Okay. Are you ready?"

Jasmyn spreads her feet, steadies her stance, takes a deep breath, and nods. "I'm ready."

~ 22 ~

UNCHARTED LAND

Jasmyn stands at the front of Evan's seventy-five-foot trawler yacht, gazing out toward the sea, reveling in the mixed emotions she experienced while training with Patricia. The gory visions that Patricia so accurately injected into her mind—her brother and sister crawling along the wooden planks on the pier—were frightening.

At first, Jasmyn cried out and collapsed with grief at the visions. After three more attempts, she became desensitized and simply stared at Logan's and Katarina's dead bodies as they moved. Then Patricia had them reach out for Jasmyn and call her name.

Jasmyn held her ground until her brother and sister stood up within arm's reach. She took two steps back, her breaths heavy.

Just as she was about to start panicking, Patricia shouted, "They're not real! Distinguish lies from what you know to be true. Kat and Logan are dead and buried. What you're seeing can only be a hallucination."

Jasmyn balled her fists and stood firm against the visions and finally distinguished between reality and fantasy. She blocked Patricia's magic, and the gory visions of her brother and sister vanished.

She released a long sigh of relief, and Patricia nodded proudly.

"Let's do a few more," Patricia said, "just to make sure you've got this."

Now, as the sea winds get brisker, Jasmyn zips her fleece sweater up to her neck and tucks her cap over her ears. She pulls out her phone and sees a message from Brian: a photo of him eating a bagel and pointing at a sign that reads, *Best Bagels in the World*.

She smiles as she types.

Jasmyn: I would give anything for a bagel right now. They only had coffee, tea, and small pastries at the hotel.

Brian: I read that the UK doesn't have good bagels. Too bad. Have you seen any castles?

Jasmyn: Ryland lived in one, but there were rats and a rotting carcass. Pretty disgusting.

Brian: Where are you now?

She snaps a photo of the front of the boat with the ocean horizon in the background and sends it to him.

Jasmyn: On our way to the Isle of Enid. It's cold and windy. Wish you were here.

Brian: Looks nice. I wish I was there too. I miss you.

Jasmyn: I miss you too.

Her last message fails to go through. She tries sending it twice more, but her phone returns connection-failure messages. After one more failed attempt, she moans with frustration, shuts off her phone, and jabs it into her sweater pocket.

She makes her way toward the half deck at the back and sits on a cushioned bench next to Gustavo. Evan stands in the middle of the group, telling a story.

"And then Gus pulls me from behind the gunner, my leg shattered below my knee, and flips me over his shoulder." Evan gestures as if lugging an invisible sack of potatoes over his broad shoulder. "He carries me all the way to his truck while the rest of the platoon gives cover. It was like, what, a hundred feet?"

Gustavo smirks. "He's exaggerating. It was fifty feet or so."

"All I remember is a lot of gunfire, a lot of shouting, and a lot of pain. They attacked our convoy hard, and we were lucky to make it out of there alive." He squeezes Gustavo's shoulder. "If it weren't for him, I'd be dead. A true-blue hero, this one is."

Gustavo blushes under Evan's spotlight, and Jasmyn can't help but smile at his shyness. Even though she doesn't really know anything about his military life, the way Evan expresses his gratitude gives Jasmyn a deep sense of pride in her uncle.

"And then"—Evan widens his eyes and looks directly at Jasmyn—"you won't believe what your uncle does."

"Oh boy, here it comes." Gustavo stands and looks away, his arms crossed.

Evan glances at Gustavo, grins, and addresses the group. "About halfway to the truck, he drops his knife, and throws me flat on the ground to go back for it!"

"What?" Patricia says. "Why?"

"It's my great-grandfather's knife," Gustavo says. "He made it himself—the steel blade, the snake handle, and the leather holder. I couldn't leave it there. That blade has been in my family for generations, and I want to pass it on to future generations. It's a family heirloom. It's priceless."

"Why would you carry a priceless heirloom on a

deployment?" Patricia asks, perplexity on her face.

"It's good luck. My grandmother had it blessed by a bishop and a cardinal in Mexico. It brought me luck in Afghanistan." He glares playfully at Evan. "It saved your ass, didn't it?"

"It sure did." Evan chuckles. "Do you still have it?"

"Of course."

In a smooth motion, Gustavo pulls out a blade from a hidden pocket. The move is so natural that it makes him seem lethal. He turns it, blade down, and hands it to Jasmyn. "I always have it on me."

"Always?" Jasmyn asks in an astonished tone, taking hold of the leather handle.

Gustavo nods. "Always."

The blade seems to hum in her hands, as if there is magic buried deep within the steel, within the wholesome belief in its blessing, a family relic passed down from generation to generation.

Maybe there is something to believing in the myth, in the giver's true intention, or maybe it really was touched by something spiritual.

She passes the knife to Patricia and senses that Patricia also feels the blade's magic. After Regina inspects it, holding it carefully and glancing at her coven sisters with wide eyes, she hands it back to Gustavo. He slides the blade into its sheath.

Evan clears his throat. "So, he drops me and runs back about twenty feet to pick up the knife. A bullet grazes my head"—he points at a scar on his right ear—"and then he runs back, picks me up, and continues running." He shakes his head. "I swear, I wanted to kill him."

As the two men laugh, Jasmyn can sense the sincerity of their friendship. Her uncle always seemed noble in the way that uncles are perceived by their nieces and nephews, but she's never once considered his time in the military, and at war, as a defining part of his personality or as something that impacted other people. Being in the military was an abstract dimension of her uncle's life, just another attribute, like the color of his hair or the fact that he likes baseball.

As she hears another veteran speak so generously of him, only now does Jasmyn understand why Patricia always comments on how amazingly blue his aura is.

She is reminded of something her grandmother used to say: "Pure goodness is hard to find. It is rare. But, when you do find it, you will never mistake it for anything else. You will know it in your heart."

That is what both Patricia and Regina saw when they first met Gustavo and encountered his blue aura, and that is what Jasmyn sees now.

The boat slows down, and the engines quiet. The navigator steps out of the control room and appears at the half deck, holding a map. "We're here, Captain."

Evan's exuberant expression grows serious. He takes his map and points to the circle Jasmyn drew, with a point in the center. "You're sure this is the spot?"

Jasmyn nods. "I recall it from Caderyn's memories, from a map he used to sail to the Isle of Enid."

Evan addresses the navigator. "Let's maintain this position for a bit."

When the navigator returns to the control room, Evan takes a deep breath and looks at Gustavo. "I'm not a huge believer in sea mythology, tales of gods and monsters and what have you, but I do have great respect for Mother Nature and these waters. We're pretty far out, so, whatever you have to do, let's get it over with so we can be on land before nightfall."

Gustavo nods and glances at Jasmyn, Patricia, and Regina.

They all rise and head to the front of the boat.

The North Atlantic winds blow Jasmyn's hair away from her face. She recalls the spell Caderyn used to hide the Isle of Enid, and the counterspell that will make it reappear.

She clasps her hands into a fold and closes her eyes. The old Norse words fall from her lips easily, and, as if she's done this before, she lifts her hands toward the sky and repeats the spell. Upon the third and final time, she opens her eyes and sees an island in the distance.

She spins on her feet and smiles widely at Gustavo. When she turns back around to face the island, Gustavo grins and walks back to Evan.

Evan shakes his head. "Well, now I've seen everything. I don't know how I'm going to explain this one at the marina."

"If all goes as planned, there won't be a lot of time or need to explain anything."

"Right," Evan says. "The time-reversal spell. It really is a hell of a story, brother. If it weren't for those dragons on the news, I'd have thought you'd gone crazy."

"Trust me." Gustavo chuckles. "If I weren't in the middle of it, I'd have thought I was crazy too."

At that exact moment, Evan catches Regina's gaze, and she bats her eyelashes at him. Evan smiles back and bows his head slightly. As if an icy wind blew across his back, he shakes his entire body, then regains his composure.

He leans in close to Gustavo. "Tell me, is Regina single?"

Gustavo smiles grandly. "She'll have you wrapped around her finger."

Evan stuffs his hands in his pockets and sighs at the prospect. "Yeah . . . I don't think I would mind being wrapped around her finger."

23

BIRTH OF A DRAGON

Seconds after Jasmyn removes the mystical cloak on the Isle of Enid, exposing it to the rest of the world, Doramae and Loritida gasp. Since their awakening, neither sorceress has felt the magical pull that guides them home to the Isle of Enid.

Until now.

They both face away from the firepit, toward Iceland's southeast horizon.

"What is it?" Ryland asks. "What's happened?"

Loritida doesn't turn to look at him. "When I awoke, I couldn't feel the Isle of Enid calling."

"Neither could I," Doramae says, her eyes narrowed toward the sea.

"But now I feel its pull." Loritida steps forward.

"You do?" Ryland inhales sharply. "They must have figured out a way to undo Caderyn's blood spell. This can't be good."

Loritida and Doramae turn to face him with puzzled looks.

Ryland swallows hard. "When I learned that the time-reversal magic only works on the Isle of Enid, Caderyn hid the island with a cloaking spell to make sure Agatha would never find it. He wanted to make sure she, or anyone from your coven, would never execute the spell again. But . . . if you two can now sense the island's location, then . . ."

"So can Jasmyn," Loritida says, eyes wide.

Doramae's heart races as she foresees the events of the

next few hours. She envisions Jasmyn reaching the Isle of Enid and somehow figuring out the time-reversal spell and reversing time, perhaps by only a few weeks, maybe by a few years. Doramae will go back to being Doramae Forester, a freelance painter from London, unaware of her true history and identity, unable to form any true relationships or bonds with anyone she meets, living a lonely, meaningless, unending, unexplained existence.

When Doramae looks up at Loritida, she can tell her cousin is having a similar epiphany.

The loud roar of a truck draws Loritida and Ryland's attention as Joseph and Oregon drive within twenty feet of them. Joseph jumps out of the driver's seat and hurries toward them.

Doramae stares at the ground, devising a plan, ignoring the bright headlights pointing right at her. When Joseph is within a foot of her, a force emanating from his enchanted charm gently pushes her back. She gasps quietly but maintains her composure.

A protection amulet! That's why Loritida's spell didn't work.

She huffs and glances at Ryland and Loritida, who are planning next steps with Joseph.

And neither of you can sense it? I would expect it from a seer with no powers, but not from you, Loritida. You are weaker than I thought.

As Ryland tells Joseph to prepare his boat for their next stop, Ryland casually places his hand on Loritida's back. Doramae shakes her head in disappointment and narrows her eyes.

He has you under his control. How can I trust you will keep your word? How can I trust that you'll be able to convince the coven, let alone kill Finna? No. I need to do this myself. I need to go back and look out for myself and Moran. I can't trust you.

"We don't have time to sail there." Doramae's

interruption draws everyone's attention. "We have to birth this dragon egg. It will get us there faster, and it will help us against Patricia."

"I've tried using Joseph's life to give life to the egg, exactly as the spell in the Book of Sol details." Loritida shrugs. "The spell doesn't work."

Holding back the urge to roll her eyes, Doramae presses her lips together and softens her face. "Loritida, perhaps Ryland was right."

Ryland straightens his back and raises his chin.

Of course flattery would work with you. Doramae keeps her concerned gaze upon her cousin. "Maybe you're not strong enough. I can execute dark magic with ease. I'll birth the dragon egg."

"But . . ." Ryland nervously glances at Doramae and back at Loritida. "You won't be able to communicate with the dragon. Only Doramae will have access to its mind."

"Don't worry." Loritida takes hold of Ryland's arm and pulls him closer. "We are all on the same side. Who cares who controls the dragon as long as we reach our goal?"

He presses his lips together. "Very well." He points to the dragon egg at Loritida's feet. "Joseph, take the egg and—"

"Not yet!" Doramae cuts Ryland off. "First, I need to prepare Joseph for the spell."

With calm confidence, without waiting for Loritida's or Ryland's approval, Doramae grabs Joseph's arm and leads him to the other side of the firepit, to the point furthest away from everyone. The dying blaze releases a gray smoke that keeps them out of clear view.

"That's far enough, Joseph."

Joseph turns around and gazes at Doramae with a sad, blank look in his eyes, as if he's resigned to his fate. He inhales through his nostrils, and his wide, muscular shoulders slump when he exhales through his mouth. "What do you want me to do?"

"Show me the amulet around your neck," Doramae says in a low voice, so only Joseph can hear.

He furrows his brows. "I'm not wearing an amulet."

Doramae jerks her head back. "Are you saying that you don't have an amulet around your neck?"

"Aye." He pulls his wool sweater down as proof, and the old, worn metal practically sparkles in the twilight. "See? No amulet."

The tips of her fingers burn when she raises her hand toward Joseph's neck, as if she's placed them on a lit stove. She closes her hand into a tight fist. A grunt escapes her.

I've never seen such protection magic. It's so potent, so permeating, that Joseph doesn't even know it exists. Even he can't remove it!

"My mistake." Doramae huffs. "Stay here. I'll be right back."

Gaze aimed at the ground, Doramae stalks back to Loritida and Ryland and, with lightning speed, constructs a plan.

When she looks up, the sight of Ryland and Loritida standing side by side churns her stomach. Spit forms in her mouth, but she swallows it back and softens her expression once more. She can't show any disdain. She needs Ryland to trust her.

Right before she reaches them, she glances over at Oregon, who is watching everything from the truck twenty feet away. She twists her fingers and conjures up a bout of chest congestion that makes Oregon hack boisterously.

Alarmed by the sudden onset of coughing, Ryland runs to the truck and opens the passenger door. He reaches in with both arms, leans his old friend forward, and pats Oregon's back to ease his discomfort.

"There, there, Oregon. You can't die on me now."

"I'm sorry, my lord. I don't know what's come over me."

Oregon coughs twice more, and Ryland hands him some water.

While Ryland's attention is occupied, Doramae grabs Loritida's arm and pulls her to the other side of the firepit.

"What are you doing?" Loritida demands, whipping her arm out of Doramae's grip.

"Joseph has a protection amulet that none of us can remove." Doramae glances back to make sure Ryland is still tending to Oregon. "That's why your spell didn't work on him. We have to use Ryland to birth the dragon,"

Loritida steps back, agape, and glares at Doramae from head to toe. "No!"

"We don't have much choice. We're running out of time. Jasmyn is probably halfway to the Isle of Enid, if not already there."

Loritida glances over her shoulder at Ryland. She turns back to Doramae and frowns. "He will never agree to this."

"We don't need his permission!" Doramae barks, but then regains her composure, holding back her frustration at her weak cousin protecting an even weaker elder.

"I . . . I can't betray him." Loritida blinks wildly. "He rescued me. He loves me. He—"

"I'll do it, then. I'll execute the spell."

"It's still a betrayal. He will hate me for letting you."

Doramae notices Ryland staring at them. She wiggles her fingers, and Oregon bursts into another coughing fit, distracting Ryland.

She glares at Loritida and speaks in a rush. "When we succeed and you two are together, this one decision won't matter. When we go back in time, Ryland won't remember a thing. And if he does, or if he sees it in his visions, he will realize we had no other choice."

"I can't." Loritida shakes her head, though with less conviction. "There has to be another way."

"There's no time to come up with another plan!" Doramae says sternly, looking past Loritida to make sure no one else hears. She sighs. "I need you on board with me. I need you on my side. I don't need another enemy. This is the only chance we have against Patricia and Jasmyn."

They stare at each other in silence.

"Do you want to change the past or not?" Doramae whispers.

With her eyes closed, Loritida presses her lips together and nods. "Fine. Execute the spell."

"Ryland!" Doramae shouts. She flicks her fingers, and Oregon breathes normally again. "We're about to begin. Please bring the dragon egg."

Ryland pats Oregon on the back one last time. Once he sees the old man is breathing well, Ryland returns to the dragon egg, hauls it up from the ground, and cradles it in his arms. With several grunts, he carries the heavy, oblong object around the firepit.

To avoid Ryland, Loritida and Joseph walk around the other side of the firepit and head to the truck. They both get inside—Loritida in the back and Joseph in the driver's seat—and wait for everything to unfold.

Ryland concentrates so hard on balancing the dense egg that he doesn't notice when Doramae lifts her hands to take aim.

In three seconds, she shouts a spell and extends her palms toward him. A bright beam of white light flows from her hands and hits Ryland and the dragon egg simultaneously, lifting them in the air before they slam hard into the center of the firepit.

A pillar of flames roars a hundred feet into the sky, and an earthquake thunders through all of Iceland. A shock wave blasts out from where Ryland previously stood, knocking Doramae to the ground.

The truck rumbles.

Oregon gasps aloud. "What happened? Ryland!" He reaches for the door.

"Silence!" Loritida hisses, murmuring a spell to make Oregon sleep.

He slumps against the window, unconscious.

Once the dust clears enough to see the road, Loritida commands Joseph to drive them down the hill, away from the chaos.

Doramae watches them drive around the boulder and out of sight. Then a miniscule growl emanates from the center of the fire behind her. A shock traverses her entire body, and she slowly turns to face the sound.

As the smoke clears, a lizard-looking animal stumbles out of the flames. It's covered in ash and soot, and it twists its torso and repeatedly falls to its side and lurches back up. It grumbles and whines as its neck, legs, arms, and tail stretch and grow rapidly, transforming it from a harmless reptile to a creature the size of an ox, then an elephant, then a whale. It continues to expand to the size of a hundred-year-old oak, creating a shadow that nearly covers the hill. Slowly, it gains stability in its front and back legs and stretches its neck into the sky.

Doramae stumbles away from the enormous beast as it raises its front legs and stomps the ground. The leaves shake off the bushes at the top of the hill, and the rocks at her feet bounce against the dirt. She runs up the hill and reaches the edge of a cliff that overlooks a long dive into a shallow ravine.

Having nowhere else to go, Doramae turns around to face

the monster she's created.

Ryland, I know you can hear me. Please, calm down, Doramae says in her thoughts, looking up at the dragon.

He jumps and stomps his enormous feet, forcing her closer to the edge. With his eyes shut, he growls and shakes his head in choppy, uncoordinated movements.

Doramae? My gods, what's happened to me? What have you done?

Doramae stands with her hands raised, staring right at the dragon. *Ryland, stop moving and listen to me!*

The dragon pauses, all four of his feet planted firmly on the ground. Several long, thick breaths later, he tilts his gigantic head up, eyes still closed.

You did this to me, Doramae. You did this to me!

Ryland, please. I am trying to help you.

The dragon huffs and lowers his head.

I have merged animals with humans before, during the Scyngar battle. Trust me, the sooner you relax and accept your new body, the sooner you will have full control of it.

Relax? He snorts. *You transformed me into a dragon!*

I had no other choice. Joseph has an impenetrable protection amulet. We had no time to get another sacrifice. Please, don't fight me. The sooner you acclimate to your new body, the sooner we can travel to the Isle of Enid, take Jasmyn's heart, and go back in time. But first, you must relax.

A low growl rises from within his chest and grows into a ferocious roar. *You want me to relax?*

And learn your new form, she replies. *You are now a dragon. You have a dragon body. You have a tail and wings and can blow fire from your snout. You must learn how to control it all. But you must first accept that you are now a dragon.*

Doramae waits nervously, her heart pounding.

After a few labored dragon breaths, the creature lowers his head as if surrendering. His breathing steadies.

I . . . I . . . am . . . a dragon.

Yes. Just breathe, and it will all come to you.

Dragon lungs are heavy, but Ryland learns to control the rhythm of his long breaths. Slow inhales and even longer exhales allow him to feel the length of his neck and throat, the breadth of his enormous torso. His chest expands as he attempts to fill his lungs completely, and the leaves on the nearby trees rustle when he blows the air outward.

The muscles in his back stretch and bend when he lifts his tail and wiggles it left and right. When he slams the tail down, the ground trembles and a plume of dirt shoots upward. He releases a low chuff.

Doramae watches cautiously as he slowly lifts a front leg. He slams it down, and the entire hill rumbles. He lifts his other front leg and lands it, more softly. His two hind legs follow, with more control. A low growl fills the air.

You're doing good, Ryland. You'll have full control soon. Open your eyes.

He growls again, shaking his head. *I can't.*

Yes, you can. Just relax and breathe. Find the muscles.

The inability to control his eyelids vexes Ryland more than all the other changes. He raises his head in search of a light source, but he doesn't sense anything the way humans can sense light through the translucent layer of skin covering human eyes. Dragon eyelids are not translucent at all. They are solid black, made up of tiny scales that block all light.

Trust me, Ryland. You will get this.

Like an uncoordinated newborn baby, Ryland tries to move the muscles in his face, but instead his tail swings left and right and obliterates a large boulder. He releases a roar as he learns

144

the mechanics of his new limb and, decisively, with control, slams his tail on the ground.

Good. That was good, Ryland. Keep going.

After a few moments, Ryland finally identifies the muscles that control the sheet of scales covering his eyes. He breathes in deeply, holds his head low, and contorts his face. When the eyelids open, he lets out a long chuff.

Raising his head toward the sky, he sees hues of blue and orange, blurry lines blending the two colors. After a few seconds, the mountains on the horizon become clearer, the setting sun sharpens, the evening stars give their first twinkles. He blinks slowly and repeatedly and releases a long, warm breath.

He lowers his head to search for Doramae and finds a woman the size of a mouse standing in front of him. Anger stirs in his stomach, and he can feel hot liquid boiling in the glands in his neck. He releases a growl, more intense than before, drops his head closer to Doramae, and takes a whiff of her scent.

Doramae holds her hands ready in defense. *Ryland, I know you're angry with me, but please understand that we need to work together. All of us. Loritida and I are in your debt for this sacrifice, but it had to be done. There was no other way.*

He lets out low, menacing growl. *Loritida agreed to this?*

She sees the logic. She knows you will eventually understand.

You manipulative snake. You pitted her against me. You've clouded her mind and her judgment.

Doramae snorts and shakes her head. *You and I both know Loritida is weak. She didn't even detect the protection spell on her own manservant! I can't rely on her alone to go up against Patricia and Jasmyn. Without you, we don't stand a chance.*

A hot breath flows from his nostrils, blowing Doramae's hair back. She closes her eyes and lifts her right hand to shield her face from the heat.

After a few silent seconds, another grumble fills the air.

This will work for all of us, she insists. *We will all go back in time and live the lives we wanted, the way we wanted. And once we go back, you won't remember a thing—as if this never happened.*

He growls once more. *That one fact is the only thing keeping me from crushing you.*

24

HOMECOMING

Setting foot on the Isle of Enid wasn't as dramatic as Jasmyn expected. On the boat ride, Patricia and Regina spoke of a powerful connection to the island, a sense of oneness with the trees and the mountains and all things natural. As Jasmyn sloshes through the shallow waters near the beach, she wonders when those feelings will kick in.

Gustavo and Evan pull the raft ahead of everyone, dragging it toward some large rocks to prop it on its side. Jasmyn spots a downed tree on the beach and heads for it, with Patricia and Regina following behind. When she sees the majestic, ice-capped peaks in the middle of the island, she pauses for a few seconds and gawks at the view.

Stuck in a daze, she imagines herself falling off the snowiest mountaintop, the highest point. She huffs and shakes her head.

Of course I imagine doom. Why can't I ever imagine victory?

Patricia and Regina walk past her and sit against the tree trunk. Patricia unzips a waterproof bag containing towels, socks, and shoes. She distributes them to Jasmyn and Regina.

"I'm a little disappointed," Jasmyn says with a frown, drying her feet with a towel.

"Why?" Patricia asks.

"Well, you two spoke of how you feel a connection with the island." She shrugs her shoulders. "I haven't felt anything yet."

"Really?" Regina squeezes water out of her floral-print dress. "You don't feel the mountains calling to you, asking you to climb them, or that patch of grass over there inviting you to lie down upon it and sleep?"

"Nope."

"You don't hear the evergreens singing their melodies?"

"Oh, come on, Regina." Patricia chortles. "Not everyone can hear tree melodies."

"Do you feel all those things?" Jasmyn asks Patricia.

"Not all of it, but some. Probably not as profoundly as Regina does. She's more carefree, more accepting of people and nature and . . . pretty much everything."

Regina throws her towel into Patricia's bag and smiles, then spins on her bare feet, her arms stretched out to the sides. "I accept everything the universe gives me."

"Stop wasting time and put on your boots. Evan packed you a pair of fleece leggings."

"Oh, good," Regina says as she digs in Patricia's bag. "It was getting a bit cold there."

Patricia rolls her eyes and glances at Jasmyn. "It took me time to communicate with nature. Not everyone is an open book. So, don't worry. It will come to you when it comes to you."

Jasmyn nods.

"And, if you're as lucky as Regina, you'll actually get visions."

Regina tilts her head. "You've never had visions?"

"Not really," Patricia says. "I've heard whispers, but I've never had nature give me visions outside of a location spell."

"Why does nature choose you more often than Patricia?" Jasmyn asks Regina.

The ocean winds blow in and brush up against Regina's body. Her dress flows forward in front of her, and her hair whips out. Patricia and Jasmyn put up their hands to block the strong breeze, but Regina giggles and allows the gust of wind to guide her to the beach grass a few feet away. She runs her hands over the tops of the stalks.

After a few seconds, she whispers something to the grass and strolls back to Patricia and Jasmyn. "It's not that I'm chosen . . . nature wants to communicate, even with those who are as guarded as Patricia. She wants to be heard, understood, respected. Let me give you a scenario to demonstrate."

Regina takes a seat on a large rock opposite Jasmyn, her dress flowing delicately over her knees. "Imagine you walk into a room and there are two people sitting in separate chairs. One has their arms and legs crossed and looks angry, and the other stands and smiles and stretches out her hand to greet you. Who would you choose to communicate with?"

"Why am I angry?" Patricia asks, lips pursed.

"Okay, not angry . . . serious. Or so distracted that you don't even notice that someone just walked into the room. The point is that they're not as welcoming as the other person, not as receptive." She glances at Jasmyn. "Who would you choose to communicate with?"

Jasmyn nods in understanding. "Sorry, Patricia."

"Oh, don't mind me, I'm too angry to care." Patricia yanks on a dry pair of socks and jams her feet into her boots. She tugs at the laces as she ties them.

Regina clicks her tongue. "It's not that you're angry, or preoccupied, or busy with other things. It's that you don't give nature's presence priority." She shrugs. "And so, nature won't give you priority, either."

Patricia waves the words away. "Whatever. It used to bother me, but I'm used to it. I have Regina to communicate with nature."

"And I have you to throw giant boulders for me," Regina says with a big smile. She turns to Jasmyn. "Don't worry. You'll feel nature's touch eventually, the way only you can feel it. And when you do, you'll see why it was so hard to explain. Like trying to describe being in love, or having children, or losing a loved one. Someone who hasn't been through it will never know how it truly feels, no matter how you explain it."

As Jasmyn ties the laces of her hiking boots, she recalls Katarina's endless supply of positivity and hope. Optimism was Kat's strength—she was always singing and dancing as if she hadn't a care in the world. Logan's strength was his fairness. He never took sides in an argument between his sisters, or between Jasmyn and her parents, and he never blamed Jasmyn for any of this mess.

Kat, the optimist; Logan, the noble. What am I? What's my strength? I wonder how Kat or Logan would have answered that question. Her shoulders slump. *Jasmyn, the jealous. Jasmyn, the mean one. Jasmyn, the horrible.*

Her eyes redden as she thinks of other titles her brother and sister would have given her, and she fights back tears.

"Oh, Jasmyn," Regina says gently.

Although Regina doesn't know why Jasmyn is getting emotional, she sits next to her against the tree trunk and gives her a sideways hug. She signals Patricia, and Patricia puts her arm around Jasmyn's other shoulder. Their warm vibrations, their love, their hope tingle all over Jasmyn's skin.

The strength in their sisterhood will complement Jasmyn's weakness—her resentment toward herself—and Jasmyn closes her eyes and accepts it.

Gustavo and Evan arrive at the tree, and the three women wipe their eyes and regain their composure.

"Everyone okay?" Gustavo asks in a cautious tone.

They nod in unison.

"Provisions for the night." Evan hands each of them a backpack. "My crew will stay aboard the ship. They're just a quick call away if we need anything. Also, that large swell we felt out in the ocean . . . that was from an earthquake in Iceland. We just heard the initial reports on the radio."

"An earthquake?" Patricia asks. She glances at Regina and Jasmyn, then back at Evan.

"Iceland is on the Mid-Atlantic Ridge." He shrugs his shoulders. "Tremors are common."

"But you said *earthquake*, not *tremor*. Which one was it?"

Evan tugs his radio from his hip and chats with a crew member. He clips the radio back in. "They'll find out more details and let us know, but I wouldn't worry."

Patricia purses her lips and looks directly at Regina.

Regina nods. In a matter of seconds, she drops her backpack, pulls off her boots, socks, and leggings, and runs toward the water.

"What is she doing?" Evan asks, squinting.

Patricia sighs. "She's seeing if the earthquake is something we need to worry about."

25

STRENGTH AND WEAKNESS

After trekking up a slight incline through the forest for forty-five minutes, they come upon a flat clearing filled with cottages. The dilapidated houses have degraded from years of neglect, and the pebbled streets are littered with discarded belongings and sprouting weeds.

"I see the bell tower!" Patricia shouts.

She speeds her pace along the unkempt trail leading toward the center of the village. She heads straight to a large wooden building with a black metal bell hanging inside a steeple.

As she arrives at the meeting house, she gawks up at the gambrel roof that is still completely intact. Though the outer walls of the building are covered in layers of green ivy and the wood shutters are barely hanging on their hinges, the structure remains sound. Gustavo and Evan drop their bags at a stone wall that stretches out from the meeting hall and encloses a garden.

Jasmyn walks up to Patricia.

"I can't believe it's still standing," Patricia says as she reaches out to touch the rectangular iron handle on one of the two panel doors.

Regina arrives next to them and drops her backpack. "I still can't believe I couldn't see anything in the water."

"Maybe it was just a tremor," Jasmyn says, setting her backpack next to Regina's.

Regina shakes her head. "My gut tells me it had something to do with Loritida or Doramae, or both. What if they're working together? What if Doramae blocked my vision?" She gasps aloud. "They can locate the Isle of Enid now that Jasmyn has removed the cloak. What if they're on their way here?"

"The cloaking spell"—Patricia turns to Jasmyn—"can you hide the island again?"

"It won't work while we're on the island."

Patricia glances back at Regina, who still looks worried. "Help Jasmyn communicate with nature. Now that we're on the island, perhaps nature will give you some insight into Agatha's magic and the time-reversal spell. I'll ask Evan to keep his crew on alert. If they see something, or someone, they'll contact us right away."

Regina nods, her eyebrows still arched in concern. She points behind the meeting house. "We'll be over there."

After Regina and Jasmyn leave, Patricia returns to the towering panel doors to the meeting hall. The hinges creak as she slowly pushes the door open and walks inside. The setting sun peeks in through the slits of shutters on the left side of the large hall, casting streaks of yellow light across the vast room. Patricia finds a dried torch on a stand, pulls it down, and lights it.

Dirt and moss cover the floor, and bugs scatter with each step she takes. Tables and chairs made of wood and iron sit in a neat formation beneath metal chandeliers that hang from hooks anchored into the supporting beams. Half-burned white candles sit in their individual holders.

As she wanders across the meeting hall, Patricia hears the distant laughter of people at a wedding dinner, the musical celebration of a newborn child, the shouts of a debate over a controversial law, and other voices and sounds that were commonplace when she lived on the Isle of Enid. A knot forms in her throat as more memories flash through her mind.

A small wooden doll sitting in a ray of sunlight on the

floor catches her attention. The bright blue and red paint of its clothes and the happy face painted on its round head conjures up innocent giggles of small children. She picks it up, smooths off the grime, and recalls all the children in her memories to track the doll's owner. After a few seconds, Patricia sighs with melancholy.

Although so much time has passed, it feels as though *no* time has passed. Her chest aches. Time is never-ending, trivial, heartless—an absolute torture to someone like Patricia who lives forever and remembers every awful detail of every gut-wrenching memory. She's spent the last few centuries in agony and bitterness, reliving her failures and reopening half-sealed emotional wounds over and over.

She would have done anything to possess a power like Agatha's, to go back and change the past, to start over.

She scowls at the far end of the room, at the stage on which Agatha stood the day before the Gregorn Dragons' first attack. The hall was filled with families several generations deep, celebrating a marriage. Agatha congratulated the couple and gave a speech about family and community, completely unaware that the dragons that once protected them against the Foreman Clan were plotting a revolution for that very night.

Spit forms in Patricia's mouth. She squeezes the wooden doll and swallows.

You had the ability to undo everything, to go back and fix what was broken, to heal us. We could have gone back to that day—the day before the beginning of the end. We could have stopped it all . . . and you chose not to.

Tossing the doll onto a nearby table, Patricia takes a few slow steps backward, glaring at the spot where Agatha stood before the entire island burned to the ground. She storms out of the meeting hall, each step full of determination.

I'll make sure Jasmyn executes your spell. I'll make sure

she heals. I'll make sure she fixes what she broke. Not for you, Agatha. Not for me. But for Jasmyn. She doesn't deserve to suffer for eternity for the choices you made. She deserves better.

~ ~ ~

Jasmyn faces the sunset, sitting crisscross in a small patch of wild grass. The fading rays blanket her face. Holding freshly picked wildflowers in her right hand, she closes her eyes, holds her left hand open with the palm facing the ground, and recites the spell once more.

> We all come from one source,
> from one source we came.
> We all feel the same pain,
> the same life, and the same death.
> Hear me now, and I will hear you.
> Tell me what I need to know.
> Show me what I search for.
> These gifts are my thanks to you.

She opens her right hand, and the wildflowers fall onto a small pile that has been growing for several minutes. This is Jasmyn's fifth failed attempt at communicating with nature.

She opens her eyes and slams her hands on the ground in frustration.

"Ugh!" she shouts up at the sky.

"What am I doing wrong?" she asks Regina, who sits three feet to her right in the same crisscross position.

"Try not to get frustrated," Regina says halfheartedly, her eyebrows furrowed, and her lips pursed in a half-frown. "Nature will speak to us when she's ready."

"Nature's not communicating with you, either?" Jasmyn asks.

Regina shakes her head. "Shush. Concentrate."

Eyebrows wrinkling with worry, Regina looks at the evergreens at the edge of the forest, then up at the sky, then back down to the tall blades of grass. She closes her eyes and mumbles the spell under her breath. When she finishes, she opens her eyes and presses her lips into a stiff line.

Patricia arrives with two water bottles and two bags of chips from the bag of provisions. Jasmyn stands, but Regina remains sitting, hunched over, staring at the ground.

"No luck yet?" Patricia asks.

Regina snatches the water bottle from Patricia and stands up, blinking wildly. Her hands are in a clawlike shape, as if she's holding something invisible. "My gut is telling me that something is coming, and I don't know what it is." She takes a deep breath. "I'm supposed to be this supernaturalist, using the mystical aspects of nature to see and feel and learn what I need to know. It was my mother's most powerful magic, and I can't even . . ." She shakes her head. "I feel useless."

Patricia places her hand on Regina's shoulder.

"I am on the Isle of Enid! This is the most powerful I will ever be, and I feel powerless." Regina rests her hands on her hips and frowns. "If I can't see what's coming, what use am I?"

Patricia hands Regina a bag of popcorn and points toward Evan and Gustavo, who are setting up tents. "Why don't you help them set up camp? Do something easy, keep your mind occupied. Maybe it will relax you, and you'll see things more clearly."

When Regina shuffles over to Evan and Gustavo, Jasmyn says, "I don't think I've ever seen her like this."

"She's just frustrated."

Jasmyn murmurs, "Her aura is usually vibrant and

positive, but now it's gray. Her vibrations have been angry ever since we left the beach."

"She feels incompetent. Communicating with nature is one of her strongest powers—that and healing." Patricia examines the land around them. "What are the chances of that earthquake happening minutes after you uncloaked the Isle of Enid? It definitely had an ominous feel to it."

A chill zips down Jasmyn's spine, and her body trembles. She crosses her arms. "So, what do we do?"

Patricia shrugs. "There's nothing we *can* do. It's like Regina said—she communicates with nature, and I move mountains. We all have our strengths and weaknesses."

"What are mine?"

Patricia faces her squarely and smirks. "You're a newbie. You don't have any yet." She nudges her shoulder and steps toward camp. "It's getting dark. I'll help them with the fire. You just lie out here on the grass and try to let nature speak to you. Remember what Regina said—relax. Nature will speak to you when she's ready."

Jasmyn lowers herself onto the wild grass and lies flat on the ground, arms and legs spread wide. She closes her eyes and repeats the spell monotonously while envisioning Patricia moving mountains during their battle with the Foreman Clan, and Regina healing Brian in the hospital.

I know I'm a newbie, but I must have something to offer.

After a few breaths, as her thoughts drift in and out of memories from the past few weeks, a menacing image of Baronyx appears in her mind. She huffs.

Really? Baronyx—a dragon I control in an entrapment spell? You count that as a strength?

She sighs and shrugs her shoulders, her eyes still closed.

I guess it's better than nothing.

26

NATURAL FORCES

The bitter scent of dandelions tickles Jasmyn's nose.

Still lying in the grass and repeating the spell in a singsong melody, she turns her head left and catches the final rays of the setting sun over the faraway mountains. She turns to her right, plucks a single fluffy dandelion from the ground, and blows on it, sending wispy petals across the moonlight's glow. As the petals clear, Jasmyn sees the pink and blue twinkles of evening stars.

Then she hears an odd shriek in the distance.

She sits up, unsure if she heard a sound or imagined it. She glances over her shoulder to where Regina and Patricia have started a fire and are now breaking pieces of wood and throwing them into the blaze. After a few seconds, she lies back down and breathes deeply once more. When she hears the shriek again, she sits up abruptly, turns toward it, and narrows her eyes.

Although she sees nothing past the towering evergreens in the moonlight, she knows she heard something from that direction. When she hears the shriek once more, she gets up and runs toward Patricia and Regina by the roaring fire. Her heart races.

"Did either of you hear that?" she asks, flustered.

"Hear what?" Patricia tilts her head.

"A low shriek." Jasmyn runs back toward the patch of grass. "Come away from the fire and listen."

They follow her, then stop and stand completely still. A breeze brushes gently over the grass and then quiets down.

"What am I listening for?" Regina whispers.

"It sounds like an eagle." Jasmyn points out to where the treetops meet the night. "It's coming from that direction."

"Are there eagles on the Isle of Enid?" Regina asks Patricia.

Patricia shakes her head. "Maybe it was a seagull. They can travel for miles."

Gustavo joins the group. "What are we looking for?"

"Jasmyn heard something." Patricia scans the sky. "A seagull, probably."

"It wasn't a seagull," Jasmyn says sharply. "I know what a seagull sounds like. This sounded like an eagle's caw, but lower."

"Evan," Gustavo shouts toward the crackling fire. "Bring over some binoculars."

"Do you hear that sound?" Jasmyn asks, stretching her arm wide. "Listen . . . there it is . . . whoosh . . . whoosh . . . whoosh."

Evan arrives with the night-vision binoculars, and Gustavo aims them toward the mountain. "I hear the whooshing, but I still don't see anything."

Regina steps away from the group and kneels. She takes off her gloves, throws them on the ground, and pulls the sleeves of her sweater up above her wrists. She rubs her bare hands along the blades of grass and repeats a spell over and over under her breath. Patricia and Jasmyn glance over at her but do not interrupt the ritual—they both pray that whatever she is trying to do works.

After a few more seconds, a loud, clear shriek fills the air. Everyone gasps, taking a few steps back.

Regina stands up and storms toward the sound. She raises her arms, palms facing outward, and shouts at the top of her lungs with full authority, "I am a natural child born into the coven of the Isle of Enid, the daughter of Jezebel—mother, daughter, seer, and protector of all that is natural on this island. I command you to reveal yourself!"

Several seconds pass, and then another shriek, this time closer.

Regina presses her lips together, takes a deep breath, and digs her feet into the ground. "You will not use our magic to hide! I command you—reveal yourself at once!"

The whooshing grows louder.

With one last inhale, Regina roars, "Reveal . . . yourself . . . now!"

The evening sky dissolves like scattering smoke and transforms into a gigantic white dragon descending upon them. Regina gasps, her eyes wide with terror, and she steps back, mouth agape.

A second later, she bends over, wraps her arms around her waist, and falls to the ground as if struck in the pit of her stomach. She screams in agony as Patricia leaps to her side, her arms spread wide and up toward the enormous beast.

"Get behind me!" Patricia shouts to everyone.

Jasmyn kneels next to Regina, and Gustavo and Evan crouch down over them. Patricia recites a spell in an angry tone, ending with a shout. "You will not touch us! You! Will! Not! Touch! Us!"

A stream of fire emanates from the dragon's white snout and flows straight at Patricia's shield. Her mystical armor withstands the attack, redirecting the blaze to the sides. The fire spreads to the trees lining the forest and to the meeting house in the center of the village. One by one, each of the old cottage houses catch fire.

Soon, the entire village is in flames.

After a few seconds, the heat penetrates Patricia's shield, and her knees buckle. Gustavo rushes to her side and holds her waist with one hand to help her stand tall. His other hand grabs her left forearm to keep it straight.

The stream of fire subsides.

The enormous white animal hovers above Gustavo and Patricia in the night sky, each wing flap feeding the blaze.

Regina screams in agony in Evan's arms. She continues to clutch her torso, coughing and spitting blood.

Stretching out her arm, Jasmyn rummages through her backpack at the base of their camp a hundred feet away, blindly looking for the entrapment case that contains Baronyx.

"It's landing," Patricia yells, her voice shaking. "Jasmyn, we need Baronyx!"

"I'm looking for the case! I can't see anything!"

"They're getting off the dragon," Gustavo says.

Her hand still up, holding the mystical shield with Gustavo's help, Patricia looks up at the monster standing over them. "We have to release Baronyx now!"

"I found the case!"

Jasmyn whispers the spell and flips the entrapment case open on the ground, and within a second, a monstrous roar rumbles across the night. Baronyx darts down from the sky, straight onto the white dragon's back. He digs his massive claws into the white dragon's scales and easily whips the creature upward.

The white dragon flips several times before regaining control, and hovers over the forest fire facing Baronyx. Without losing another second, Baronyx darts at Ryland's smaller frame.

Ryland uses his tail and legs to resist Baronyx's attack, and both creatures twist in the air, wings flapping wildly, before crashing half a mile away.

The ground shakes. Rows of trees topple like dominoes, and dust and debris fill the air.

Everyone falls to their knees.

"Jasmyn," Regina calls weakly, coughing up more blood. She reaches her arm upward while still leaning on her elbow. "The dragon . . ."

Patricia recites a spell to clear the dust and smoke and finds Regina in the firelight.

"Yes, it was a dragon." Patricia bends down to Regina. "What hurts?"

"Everything." Her voice is weak, barely above a whisper.

"Damn you and your weak shielding abilities," Patricia scolds. "I told you to work on that!"

Regina coughs. "I will work on it." She takes her index finger and crosses her heart. "I promise. The dragon . . ."

"Don't worry about the dragon. Baronyx is taking care of it."

"Her legs look broken," Evan says. He swallows hard. "Her arms too. It's like she was crushed, but I've been with her the whole time. I didn't see anything hit her."

"No . . . Doramae . . ." Regina whispers. Patricia leans in to listen better. "Doramae is . . . powerful. The dragon . . ." Regina presses on her stomach and groans in agony.

"You think she's powerful?" Patricia scowls and stands tall, her hands balled into fists. "Well, so am I!"

Before another second passes, Patricia spreads her hands, her fingers stretched apart, and storms toward Loritida and Doramae. Scooping her hands in front of her and then curling them in as if she's holding a basketball, Patricia elevates the ground beneath Loritida and Doramae and sends boulders and downed trees flying at them.

Patricia steadies her stance and closes in on the mystical ball in her hands, attempting to touch her fingertips together to crush the two sorceresses in a sphere of debris, but she can't push through their combined resistance.

Jasmyn yells as a cascade of boulders thunders toward Patricia. In a blink, Jasmyn lifts her arms and uses all the energy in her body and mind to generate a shield over Patricia. The boulders crash down upon the shield, saving Patricia but knocking both of them off their feet. Patricia loses her hold on Loritida and Doramae.

Patricia and Jasmyn stand and run to the cliffside that was created when Patricia tore up the earth.

"That's Doramae," Patricia says through seething teeth. "Aim for her."

Just as Patricia trained her, Jasmyn raises her arms, curls her fingers toward a nearby mountain, and breaks the ancient rock into several hundred enormous boulders. With a hard swing of her arms and torso, she shoots the bombardment at Doramae.

As Jasmyn showers Doramae with an onslaught of bedrock, Patricia forms another sphere and lifts the two sorceresses off the ground. After a deep inhale, Patricia flexes every single muscle in her body, releases a massive roar, and squeezes the sphere with all her might until her hands finally clasp together.

An earsplitting explosion is heard for miles, and a thick plume of dirt fills the air. The monumental impact generates a forceful wind that knocks Jasmyn off her feet. She hits the back of her head on a stone on the ground and blacks out.

Everything is silent. The ground shakes. Jasmyn can't move.

A voice speaks in her head. *Oh, my dearest Jasmyn.*

Regina? I can't see anything. I can't move. Why can't I move?

Regina continues, *Shush, and listen. I don't have much time.*

Don't have much time? Why? What's happening? Panic claws at Jasmyn.

Just be quiet and listen!

As Regina whispers in her mind, Jasmyn opens her eyes and sees Gustavo kneeling overhead, wearing something over his eyes and shining a blue light in her face. Gustavo's mouth moves slowly, but Jasmyn doesn't hear a word. She doesn't hear the fire burning behind him or the crackle of hundred-year-old trees falling. She doesn't feel her uncle pick her up and carry her over rocks and downed trees to safety. She doesn't feel blood dripping from the back of her head, or the two broken ribs in her chest.

She closes her eyes, and she can almost feel Regina's hand cradling her face.

There. I've told you all that I know. I've healed you, but now you need to rest. You'll need your energy later. Promise me you'll rest, Jasmyn.

I promise.

It's time for me to go.

Where are you going?

Don't worry. Just rest.

Regina's voice fades into the distance as Jasmyn's mind grows quiet. She can sense Regina healing her, sending her good vibrations and intentions. She feels Regina's love, and it calms her.

Don't go. Jasmyn whispers in her mind, almost unconscious.

I must. It's time.

Jasmyn whimpers and falls into a deep sleep.

But I will always be with you. Remember that. We are all connected. You, me, Patricia . . . the universe . . . we are all connected.

27

REINFORCEMENTS

"My legs," Loritida whimpers, dangling over Doramae's shoulder. "I can't feel them."

"Hang on." Doramae grunts at the weight of carrying her cousin. "We're almost there."

Patricia's magical sphere had indeed collapsed inward, but Doramae manipulated the force of the implosion to propel herself and Loritida away from the blast site, sending them several miles across the island, to the northern shore.

When they reach the coast, Doramae drops Loritida, letting her roll clumsily in the sand. Doramae lands smoothly on her feet.

With a twist of her hands, Doramae uproots a tree at the edge of the beach and breaks the trunk into several chunks of wood. She throws them into a neat pile and whispers a spell to light it.

After three attempts at pushing herself to her knees, Loritida drops onto her hip and slams her fists on the ground. "That bitch Regina did this to me."

"She wasn't as unskilled as you thought." Doramae glances sideways at her.

Loritida whips her hair away from her face. "I killed her, didn't I?"

"If you weren't so weak, we might have been able to kill Patricia as well. You took a single blow from a dying witch, and now look at you. Pathetic."

"How dare you," Loritida seethes.

"How dare I, indeed." Doramae glowers down at her. "So, what . . . Finna punished you, and you just accepted it? You whined and pitied yourself to complacency and made yourself weak." She points at the ground and yells, "I would never have put myself into a deep sleep like you did. I would never have allowed myself to become so vulnerable, like you."

Inch by inch, Loritida rises to her knees, then her feet. With her back straight, shoulders square, and eyes narrowed upon her cousin, she stands tall and speaks in a strong, steady, dominating tone. "You know nothing of what I endured."

"I have endured plenty too." Doramae rolls her eyes and gazes at the ocean. "Now, stop whining, I have to think of—"

A gust of air shoots out of Loritida's hand, and Doramae takes a step back.

"I am not done speaking," Loritida growls.

Glaring, Doramae inhales and gives Loritida her attention.

"I am sure you had questions about your past, about your unique situation when you were traveling across the north, sailing and scaling mountains with peoples of all kinds," Loritida says as she takes a shaky step toward Doramae, her eyes severe, "but you were oblivious of your punishment. That ignorance, that naiveté, gave you hope, and made you wonder, and pushed you to explore and travel and . . . have a life. You had people, conversation, interaction, affection, human touch."

At the sight of Loritida's crimson aura, Doramae steps back.

"As for me"—Loritida moves forward—"I had no one. Not a single person to talk to. No one to hold or be held by. No one to gaze upon. No one." She lowers her gaze, takes a deep breath, and scowls back at Doramae. "And the things I did have . . . endless time, my memories, and the knowledge that Finna and my

166

coven sisters agreed to banish me . . . were unbearable. If I could, if only I were a regular person with no magical powers, I would have ended my suffering long ago. But our magic doesn't allow us to kill ourselves. I had to live, against what little free will I had left." She swallows hard again. "I had to live."

Loritida glances at the moon and closes her eyes for a second. "Year after year, decade after decade, century after century"—her bottom lip trembles and her voice cracks, but she swallows hard and regains her composure—"when the sun hit the highest point in the sky, and another year had passed, and no one had come looking for me, I was reminded of how alone I was in this world, of how trapped I was, of how empty and meaningless my life was. There was no promise of change. No hope."

Loritida looks away to hide her grimace, whispering names and curses under her breath. "The only mercy I could offer myself was sleep."

Doramae's glare softens, and her eyes turn apologetic. After a few seconds of silence, she offers, "Cousin, please forgive me, I did not realize—"

"No, cousin," Loritida says, turning to watch the flames, "you did not."

Several minutes pass with only the crackling of the fire to fill the night. Doramae bends down to poke at the blaze with a thick branch, contemplating how insane she would have gone in Loritida's shoes. To live eternally with pain and misery constantly gnawing at you, with no possibility of closure, or a moment of reprieve, or even death to end your suffering. She, too, would have chosen to sleep to avoid going mad. In fact, she finds herself amazed that her cousin is still mentally intact.

Doramae glances up at Loritida, who is now staring out towards the black ocean with her hands raised up towards the stars, reciting a spell. She promises herself that she will take revenge on

Finna for what she did to her cousin. When the faces of the other complacent women of her coven appear in her mind, Doramae snarls and pokes at the flames harder, imagining the fiery stick piercing each and every one of their eye sockets. Once she is satisfied with the imaginary massacre, she stands and tosses the piece of wood into the flames.

Loritida wobbles up to the fire. "I can feel Joseph approaching. He'll be here soon. Can you communicate with Ryland and tell him to come to this beach?"

"I can't sense him."

"What does that mean?" Loritida swallows hard. "Is he dead?"

"I don't know," Doramae replies in a gentle tone. "This is the first time I've given life to a Gregorn Dragon. I haven't had time to decipher the intricate rules of their magic. Besides, Ryland was no match for Baronyx."

"So . . . he's dead."

"We don't know that yet." Doramae gazes softly at her cousin. "In any case, I hope you were right about him."

"I am. You'll see." Loritida stares at the dark waters under the moonlight. "A man as self-interested as Ryland would never give away something as valuable as a Gregorn Dragon egg unless he had more than one."

A bright orb glows in the night, catching their attention. As the light approaches, a low, thumping sound grows louder and louder. The light shines directly on them, and a small helicopter flies over their heads, low enough to create a wind drag that nearly blows out the fire. It lands far into the beach, away from the ocean.

The cockpit door opens, and Joseph jumps out. He pulls out two duffel bags and walks over to Loritida and Doramae. The helicopter takes off, flies into the pitch-dark sky, and disappears into the night.

"You were right, my mistress," Joseph says. He places both duffel bags down and unzips them to expose the treasure. "He had four more dragon eggs."

Loritida gasps.

Doramae's eyes widen with excitement. Her gaze is glued to the shimmering outer shell of the ancient eggs.

"Can you birth more than one?" Loritida asks.

"I can," Doramae says with a vicious smirk. She lifts her gaze to Loritida. "Are you ready?"

28

FIRELIGHT

"Wake up!" Patricia shouts in Jasmyn's face.

After Patricia repeats her waking spell for the tenth time, Jasmyn finally opens her eyes. Still on her knees, Patricia releases her hands from a prayer fold and places them on the ground. Her head hangs low as she lets out a gasp and a soft whimper. She takes a deep breath and brushes her face with her sleeve before standing and stepping away.

Gustavo closes the distance to Jasmyn and chokes back a sob. He wipes her cheek with a wet cloth and cradles her face in his hand before hugging her.

"What happened?" Jasmyn coughs and chokes on the smoky air. She tries to clear her throat, but the thick haze gets stuck in her lungs when she inhales, and she coughs harder than before. After a few hacks, she spits out a mouthful of thick phlegm.

Gustavo hands her a bottle of water. "You hit your head and got knocked out."

After several long sips, Jasmyn sits up, tasting dirt on her lips. Gustavo pours water onto a clean white rag and hands it to her.

"How long was I out?"

"About forty-five minutes. Do you feel dizzy?"

She rubs her eyes and wipes her face clean of the dirt. "No."

"Do you feel pain? You hit your head pretty hard. There was blood, but I couldn't find where it came from."

Jasmyn pokes around her scalp and finds a sore spot but says nothing to her uncle. "I'm fine."

Gustavo places his hand on her cheek. "You really scared us there."

He glances at Patricia, who sits sobbing against the tree stump, her forearms resting on her knees and her head hanging low.

"Wait here," he says to Jasmyn, and she nods.

He walks to Patricia, kneels, and places his hand on her shoulder. "She's awake. It worked. Jasmyn's fine."

"Just give me a second," Patricia says, voice cracking. Slowly, she stands, walks to a boulder further away from Jasmyn, and leans against it, facing the newly created valley, ablaze with a dark-orange glow.

Gustavo follows her and places his hand on her back, whispering.

Jasmyn vaguely recalls hearing Regina whisper, "I've healed you," but she can't identify the time or place. She furrows her brows as she tries to think of the exact moment, but nothing appears in her mind. The last thing she recalls is staring at the fire, and then waking up.

The sore spot on her head throbs, and she rubs her finger against it. *Just a bump. If there was blood, there isn't any now. Regina's good. I need to learn some healing spells.*

She searches for Regina and spots her lying on the ground a few yards away, Evan at her side beneath a tree untouched by dragon fire.

Before Jasmyn stands, she glances back at Patricia and Gustavo and sees them in an embrace, Patricia's head buried in his chest.

With slow, careful movements, Jasmyn rises to her feet and leans against a downed tree. Holding the wet cloth over her mouth, she steps toward Evan and Regina. Regina's head is turned sideways, her body lying still, her red hair cascading over her shoulders and onto her chest.

Jasmyn stops abruptly.

The realization hits her like a punch to the chest, knocking the wind out of her lungs. With her mouth agape, she drops to her knees next to Regina's body.

Her bottom lip trembles, and tears spill down her cheeks. "But . . . she healed me. She told me to rest. She . . ."

Evan places his hand on her shoulder. "I'm so sorry, Jasmyn."

As sorrow overcomes her, she buries her face in her hands and sobs. Regina's last words echo in her mind. *You, me, Patricia . . . the universe . . . we are all connected.*

Regina's brilliant, positive aura that shone in every room she entered, that warmed and encouraged Jasmyn's own weak spirit, no longer exists. Her flowery dresses, her wavy red hair, her radiant smile, her endless optimism—every beautiful part of her is gone. A part of Jasmyn is now missing—the cheerful melody that has accompanied her these past weeks has been silenced.

After a few moments, Jasmyn stands, her hands balled into tight fists, and scowls up at the night sky. "How many more people must die before you give me my grandmother's magic?" she shouts. "Kat, Logan, Regina . . . who's next? Is it Patricia? My uncle? Who? Is this all part of your plan? Kill everyone I love, make me suffer everyone's death? Are you going to show me the spell once everyone is gone?"

She picks up a heavy stone and throws it with all her strength, growling as she pushes her muscles and limbs to their limit. It flies out past the valley, over half a mile away.

"Why are you doing this to me?" she cries. "Why don't you show me the time-reversal spell? Why hold out on me? Why?"

She inhales profoundly. "Why?" She closes her eyes and whimpers. "Regina didn't deserve to die. I deserve to die, not her."

She slumps onto the tree trunk, defeated. Her breath shakes as she stares at the orange hue of the fire in the valley. Her facial muscles are tired of crying, and her face is devoid of expression. She allows the tears to stream down her cheeks and onto her jacket.

I don't know the spell. I can't turn back time. I don't know anything except that Kat and Logan are dead because of my actions, and now Regina is dead because of my incompetence. I'm no sorceress. I'm a burden. An anchor. I'll take everyone down with me. If anything happens to Uncle Gus . . . or Patricia . . .

She inhales and closes her eyes tightly. *No one else should die because of me.*

"Jasmyn," Patricia says gently from behind her.

Jasmyn gasps and straightens her back. Her throat tightens even more, and it's nearly impossible to swallow.

She doesn't turn around. She can't look at Patricia; she can't look at anyone. When she feels Patricia's hand on her shoulder, she steps away without glancing back. She grimaces, crosses her arms, and takes another step further away.

"You said Regina healed you and told you to rest. Did she mention anything else?"

Jasmyn nods, still unable to look at Patricia. She takes a deep breath. "She did," she says, her voice hoarse.

"What did she say?"

A loud grumble draws Jasmyn's attention to the left side of the valley, away from the fire. The steady growl seems to call her. She follows the sound around a thick tree, closer to the cliff. Under the fading moonlight, she spots Baronyx's mighty form.

"What is Baronyx doing?" Jasmyn asks, still not looking at Patricia.

Patricia steps aside but keeps her distance. "I don't know. He came back with the white dragon and sat down there. I think he might be waiting for you."

As Jasmyn gazes at the bruised and bloodied white dragon lying next to Baronyx, she recalls everything Regina told her before she died. Regina could have healed herself but chose to heal Jasmyn instead and give her all the information she needed to continue her quest. Jasmyn's grief mixes with hope, and with a painful understanding of Regina's selfless act.

"That's Ryland," she says barely above a whisper.

Patricia steps closer and tenderly places her hand on Jasmyn's back. "I'm sorry. I didn't hear you."

After a long, deep breath, Jasmyn lifts her head, turns around and looks Patricia straight in the eyes. Although she wants to embrace her coven sister, she can't bring herself to do so. She doesn't want to be comforted. This isn't a time for mourning.

Jasmyn presses her lips into a frown and clears her throat. "The white dragon is Ryland."

Patricia gasps, and her eyes widen. She glances over at the white dragon, then back at Jasmyn.

Jasmyn continues, "And he knows how to execute the time-reversal spell."

29

DAYBREAK

The morning sun is rising in the northernmost parts of the world, and the deep-orange sky on the horizon gives Jasmyn a newfound sense of optimism.

As she scrambles down to the valley where Baronyx and Ryland lie side by side, the smoke-filled air clears behind her. Although Patricia was able to put out most of the fire and whisk away thick plumes of smoke with the wind, the unpleasant scent of burning wood had lingered. But, now, as they continue down the hillside, crisp mountain air fills Jasmyn's lungs.

The long trek gives Jasmyn time to think of all that has occurred these past few weeks, and all that will be undone. Katarina, Logan, and Regina won't be dead, the West Coast won't be in utter ruins, and thousands of people in San Francisco won't die, because the Gregorn Dragons won't be released.

As she traverses the rocky hill, she thinks about how Caderyn and the Foreman Clan will go along living out their solitary, clandestine lives, unaware of her existence. Loritida will remain in exile, and Doramae will return to being oblivious to who she really is.

Everyone who has come into her life these past few weeks won't know what has transpired—who died and who lived. Only Jasmyn will remember.

As she narrows her eyes at the white dragon, Jasmyn stops cold in her tracks and gasps.

"What's wrong?" Patricia asks as she arrives at her side.

"Ryland knows about the time-reversal spell."

"Yeah. So?"

Jasmyn places her hands on her hips. "How could he have possibly known about the spell?"

"Probably from his visions. What does it matter?"

"He knew Finna used the spell long ago. He told Caderyn to hide the island so Nana couldn't use it."

Gustavo catches up with them, his shoes scuffing the dirt.

Jasmyn continues, "What if he sees other things in his visions, like where we live and how Nana grew old and weak, and how she didn't choose a successor? What if he comes after us?"

"Maybe you should contact Patricia when you go back and tell her what's happened," Gustavo says.

"No!" Patricia glares at Gustavo, then glances at Jasmyn. "You can't tell me anything."

Jasmyn tilts her head. "Why not?"

"You just can't."

"How can I *not* tell you everything that's happened?" Jasmyn furrows her eyebrows. "We're sisters . . . aren't we?"

The island winds blow through the trees, creating a faint rustle as Jasmyn stares at her coven sister with sad eyes.

After a few silent moments, Patricia takes both of Jasmyn's hands. "I am your sister, now. I won't be when you go back. I won't even know you exist. You will mean nothing to me."

Jasmyn yanks her hands out of Patricia's hold.

Patricia continues, "There is a reason both Finna and Agatha kept the time-reversal spell a secret. It's a very powerful ability. As you have experienced, when people discover its existence, you become a target."

Gustavo shakes his head. "But you would never go after it. You would never betray Agatha."

"I have betrayed her in the past. I've abandoned Agatha

out of my own selfishness." Patricia gazes at the ground, lamenting the last time she spoke with Agatha.

Images flow through her mind: Agatha holding her newborn, Patricia walking out of Agatha's life, her dead coven sisters scattered across the Isle of Enid after the dragon rebellion. She shakes her head to make the images go away, but they bombard her, as they have repeatedly and mercilessly since Agatha died.

"There were times when, if I'd known a power like this existed, I might have gone after it. I might have fought Agatha for it. All the pain I went through, so much death and agony . . . I might have taken it from her just to go back and undo it all."

Jasmyn shakes her head and blinks back tears.

Patricia steps close to Jasmyn once again. "This is why Agatha and Finna never told anyone about their power. They kept their secret for centuries. You must respect and follow their example."

"But if you never know about everything we've gone through, how will we become . . ." Jasmyn's bottom lip trembles. She presses her lips together to keep from crying.

After a long sigh, feeling sadness that she, too, will not have the same closeness, the same sisterhood with Jasmyn, Patricia embraces her. It breaks her heart that they won't be coven sisters, not in the way they are now, and that Jasmyn will have to bear all this truth without her.

"You remember how you used to be?" Patricia whispers in Jasmyn's ear. "Angry at the world, hating everyone and everything."

Jasmyn nods in her embrace.

"I was the same, only worse. I have magic, and I have misery. Just imagine what I would do to get that power." Patricia pulls back and brushes Jasmyn's auburn hair away from her face.

"You should tell Agatha everything. She is the only person you should tell. What she decides to do, well." Patricia steps back and shrugs. "I guess we'll just have to wait and see."

A low murmur from Baronyx draws everyone's attention. The dragon stands up, looking at something past the mountains. He releases a louder grumble.

Gustavo pulls his binoculars out of his backpack and aims them in the same direction. He curses when he sees what has attracted Baronyx's attention.

"Two dragons, one black, one yellow, heading this way," Gustavo says.

"Two more dragons?" Patricia demands as Gustavo hands her the binoculars. She, too, curses. "How far away are they?"

He takes the binoculars back. "I'd estimate about a hundred miles out. They're flying, somewhat clumsily, but still, they'll cover a lot of miles in the air."

"Wait here," Jasmyn says before she darts down the valley toward Baronyx, jumping over rocks and crevices. She trips and falls, scraping her hands and knees, but stands up and continues scrambling. The ground curves into a steep dive, and she tumbles down the hill. She finishes rolling about fifty feet from Baronyx's tremendous legs.

Jasmyn looks up at the beast towering over her, blocking out the morning light, and she feels insignificant in size. He could crush her with one short step, effortlessly, before she'd have a chance to react.

She is thankful he is on her side this time.

Now that Baronyx sees Jasmyn, he shares his thoughts, showing her his battle with the white dragon. Holding Ryland's arm in his snout, Baronyx easily dragged him across the hills like a child playing with a rag doll. Although Ryland struggled against Baronyx, he wasn't strong enough to prevent Baronyx from tossing him over and over, sending him tumbling as if he had no control over his own dragon body.

Jasmyn inhales as she sees the moment when Ryland bowed his long, white neck and whimpered so pitifully that Baronyx stopped his final assault. Ryland begged Baronyx to spare his life, offered his servitude, and swore he had what Jasmyn needed.

The towering beast lowers his gaze toward Jasmyn, and she takes a few steps back. He releases a low purr.

As you have seen, this pathetic excuse for a Gregorn Dragon begged me to keep him alive. He claims he has something for you.

Thank you, Baronyx, for not killing him. I cannot speak directly to him. Will you help me communicate?

Baronyx grumbles, long and low. *Of course.*

~ ~ ~

Minutes go by as strong storm winds pick up from the east, bringing ominous gray clouds. Gustavo keeps a stern eye on the approaching dragons.

"What's Jasmyn doing?" he asks Patricia, still looking westward through his binoculars.

"They're communicating."

"She's got to hurry up." Gustavo lowers the binoculars. "The small black dragon has trouble flying, but the bigger yellow one is steadier."

Patricia purses her lips. "It's Loritida and Doramae. I'm sure of it."

After gazing at the oncoming storm, Gustavo looks through the binoculars again. "The black dragon is stumbling a lot, and the yellow one keeps returning to help it. It's slowing their progress. The wind is blowing against them, so maybe that's giving them problems too. Still, at their rate of travel, it won't take long for them to reach us."

"Just keep an eye on them. When they get close, we'll warn Jasmyn."

Gustavo sighs. "I think you're wrong about Jasmyn not telling you." He sits on a rock facing west.

"Why?"

"Because you and Jasmyn have a bond now. To deny that bond is cruel, not only for her but for you."

She sits next to him and gestures for the binoculars. He hands them to her, and she raises them to her eyes.

"It's not that I don't want to know Jasmyn," Patricia says as she stares out at the dragons. "It's just that . . . I know how I might react to such information at that moment in time."

"And how might you react?"

She lowers the binoculars and resists looking up at Gustavo. "Not well. I was an entirely different person before Agatha died. Before any of this happened."

"Before Jasmyn came into your life."

She catches his smirk.

"She changed your life once. She can do it again."

"You're missing my point." She takes a deep breath and looks straight into his eyes. "Loritida started with a good intention, and it got corrupted by power. Doramae was forced into using her magic for what she believed to be a noble reason. Both were affected by the horrible things that happened in their lives. Look at them now. They don't care about what happens to me, to Jasmyn. They will do anything, kill everyone, if it means they can go back and change their past. That could easily have been me."

"I don't believe that."

"It's true." She hands the binoculars back. "I hated the

Foreman Clan. I hated the Gregorn Dragons. I hated the universe for allowing things to happen the way they happened. To lose everyone you hold dear . . . it changes a person. They killed Loritida's daughter before her eyes. Doramae lost her husband. I lost people too. I had hatred too."

"But, by the time all of this started, you were over it, right? You're not as insane as Loritida and Doramae."

She looks away for a few seconds, then gazes up at Gustavo with sad eyes. "You never get over something like that. It burns inside of you, eats away at everything good you have left. And even when you think you might be over it, it comes back blazing, like a chronic infection that makes you feel sick and rotten. And if you're sick long enough, if you've suffered long enough, knowing it will never end . . . you'd do anything to cure it."

He shakes his head. "But you love Jasmyn. You wouldn't do anything to hurt her."

"I do love Jasmyn, now. It's the love I have for her, now, that has eased the pain and resentment. But, without it . . ."

A sense of shame hits her. Her face twists at her horrible thoughts, and she looks away. After a few seconds, she regains her composure and faces Gustavo without looking directly into his eyes.

"The only reason I haven't ripped out and consumed Jasmyn's heart myself is because I have grown to love her by going through all this chaos alongside her, helping her, guiding her, suffering with her. I grew to love Jasmyn and Katarina before I learned of the time-reversal spell. And now that I dearly love them, I can't imagine killing Jasmyn and consuming her heart. Now, I don't want the chance to go back to stop the Gregorn Dragon rebellion. Jasmyn, Katarina, and Logan may never exist if I do, and I don't want to live with that. But, if I knew about the spell without experiencing all of this, without loving them—"

"I don't believe that." Gustavo shakes his head. "There's no way you were that bad."

Storm clouds fill the dawning sky, and the wind picks up. Patricia zips her jacket to her chin, crosses her arms, and stares into the distance. "It's not about being good or bad. It's about curing the chronic infection that has been killing you inside, slowly, decade after decade, century after century. It's a chance to end the torture, to go back and fix what broke. The nightmares, the dead faces of my sisters, of their families, their children. To live with that loss, that pain, that hate. If I had the power to turn back the clock, if I knew that power existed and I could get a hold of it—"

She swallows hard to hold back her emotions.

"My love for Jasmyn, now, is what is keeping me from doing what Loritida and Doramae are doing. It's easy to just say that they're insane, but they are suffering in a way you can't imagine, and they want to make the suffering go away. And that . . . could easily have been me."

With those last words, Patricia hangs her head low, covers her face with her hands, and sobs.

Stunned at her revelation, Gustavo lets her cry for several seconds before putting his arm around her. When her body shakes from sobbing, he holds her tighter. He doesn't know whether he would despise or pity the woman Patricia might have been, but he certainly knows he loves the woman in his arms at this very moment. He loves her for sacrificing her chance at curing her own pain to allow Jasmyn to cure hers.

Patricia's sobs weaken, and she sits there in silence, in his arms, until her breathing is slow and steady.

After a few more minutes, Gustavo looks through the binoculars and sees that the dragons are still far away. He lowers them. "So, I guess there's no real future for us, then, huh?"

She chuckles softly, still unable to look into his eyes, and sighs. She wipes the tears from her cheeks. "I don't think so."

After another breath, he places his fingers on her chin, turns her face so that their eyes meet, and gives her a soft kiss on her lips. Her tears roll over their lips, and he lets a tear stream down his own cheek. After what seems like too short of a time, he pulls away and whispers, "It was now or never." He smiles. "Literally."

She chuckles once more before giving him an even longer, softer, everlasting kiss.

When she pulls away, she rests her head on his shoulder and hugs his left arm. He takes another look through the binoculars and quietly begs the heavens and stars to do what they can to keep the dragons away for just a little longer.

30

EXECUTION

And once you're at the highest point in the world, you recite that spell while your heart is pierced by a sacred knife. Although it isn't dark magic, the spell requires a life. Your own life. Only then will the spell be complete.

Jasmyn furrows her brow at Baronyx. *Tell Ryland that we can't kill ourselves. I can't sacrifice my own life.*

Then you must get someone to do it for you. Baronyx huffs, glances at Ryland, and points his snout at Jasmyn. *That is all Ryland has to say about the spell.*

Jasmyn purses her lips. *Why is he sharing the details of the spell with me now? Why should I trust him?*

The two dragons exchange gurgles and ruffs. Baronyx stares down at Ryland, and Ryland lifts his head slightly, intermittently purring and chuffing, then lowers his head.

He says he misjudged Loritida's loyalty, and he believes Doramae would kill him along with everyone else she takes revenge upon if she were to go back in time. And he says he's tired.

Jasmyn wrinkles her forehead. *Tired? Of what?*

Baronyx grumbles, then releases a short, sharp roar.

Ryland rises to his feet and circles so that he is facing westward. He nestles down and releases a loud exhale through his nostrils, followed by a few more purrs and chuffs. When his monumental body touches the ground, a cloud of dirt rises around him. He twists his long neck to gaze at Jasmyn.

Baronyx huffs. *He says he is tired of living so many*

centuries without purpose, love, or friendship. The only true friend he has ever had is Oregon. Despite knowing his true origin, Oregon has shown him friendship and love these past decades like no one else. If Ryland goes back to Loritida's or Doramae's time, centuries before Oregon was born, so many things may change in the world that he and Oregon may never cross paths. It is only now that Loritida has betrayed him that Ryland appreciates Oregon's part in his life. He is like a brother to him. It is the most important friendship of his entire existence, and he doesn't want to risk losing it.

With her hands on her hips, Jasmyn paces between the two gigantic beasts.

Is Ryland's confession a surprising revelation or part of a grander scheme? Is he lying to her, tricking her to buy Loritida and Doramae time?

She glances up at Baronyx and back down at the grass. An idea pops into her mind. She pivots on her feet and gazes up at Baronyx.

Tell Ryland to show you his vision of when Finna performed the time-reversal spell. I want to see it.

After a few seconds, Baronyx shares Ryland's vision, and Jasmyn gasps.

Her eyes widen as she watches the scene unfold in his mind, from the moment the Foreman Clan defeats the coven and are about to kill Finna until the end when Patricia plunges a sacred dagger into Finna's heart to complete the time-reversal spell.

The vision dissolves into nothing, and Jasmyn's heart races.

Please tell Ryland that I believe him, and that I will not forget this.

Baronyx stands up tall and stretches to look westward again. *Your battle is not over,* he growls.

Ryland stands up.

Jasmyn follows Baronyx's gaze and sees two flying dragons. When she looks up at Patricia and Gustavo, they are already running downhill.

When they reach her, all three of them pull out their fleece jackets, hats, and gloves.

Jasmyn commands Baronyx to spread the fingers of his right paw so that Jasmyn, Patricia, and Gustavo can climb in. Once they are snug within the folds of his mammoth fingers, Baronyx takes flight toward the icy mountains on the Isle of Enid, the highest point on the island, the highest point in the entire world.

Baronyx zooms upward, and Jasmyn shuts her eyes as the fast-moving air strikes her face. She blocks the wind with her hand. Green-and-brown patches of earth blur below her dangling feet, and she can't get a true feeling of where they are. It doesn't matter—she showed Baronyx their final destination.

"Did you get the spell from Ryland?" Patricia shouts directly into Jasmyn's ear.

Jasmyn nods. "Yes. He told me everything," she shouts back.

"Do you think we can trust him?"

Jasmyn huffs, recalling the vision he showed her, and nods again. "Definitely."

Ryland, still unaccustomed to his dragon form, attempts to take flight. His bruised wings give out as he struggles to control them. He falls to the ground, landing on his feet, and then attempts once more.

As soon as he gains control of his wings and reaches a little bit of height, he feels an anvil-like strike along his jagged spine. He plummets toward the earth as Doramae digs her claws into his back.

Tell me how to execute the spell! She locks her jaws

around his neck. *Tell me, or you will die!*

Her teeth dig into his leathery white scales until hot blood runs down his neck. The weight of Doramae's gigantic body cracks his spine, and a tingling, numbing sensation crawls up his appendages. Yet, despite being crushed by a dragon superior in size and strength, Ryland chuckles. If his dragon lips would allow, he would smirk.

You no longer have control over me, Doramae. You are done. I told Jasmyn everything. She knows what she must do.

No! Loritida growls next to Doramae. *How could you do this to me, Ryland? I'll go back to my prison. I'll be trapped again!*

You should have thought of that before offering me up as a sacrifice.

Loritida shakes her enormous head and huffs. *We had no choice.*

We've all had difficult choices to make, Loritida. Now I choose Jasmyn. In fact, I should have chosen her from the start. She is, after all, Finna's kin, and Finna was the greatest leader of your coven. In any case, Jasmyn will remember that, in the end, I chose her over you and Doramae. I chose to help her survive and save her brother and sister. I might even be in her good graces because of this one act of selflessness. And the best part . . . I will never have to see either of you ever again.

With her tail whipping and wings flapping wildly, Loritida slams her feet down on a boulder, crushing it to pieces, and roars toward Ryland. *I had to make a choice, Ryland. There was no other option!*

A sense of numbness spreads along Ryland's tail and back, and he finds it difficult to breathe. *Oh, but you did have a choice. Your dragon form is proof. What you didn't know was that I, too, had options. You see, it doesn't matter to me who executes the spell. I will live, I will survive, and sooner or later, I will learn of all that has transpired.*

Ryland coughs up blood and moans with pain. *My intention, initially, was to go back to our time together, but I didn't think you were so weak as to allow yourself to be manipulated. Doramae made you sacrifice the only person in the world who came looking for you. Trust me, that will never happen again. You will live out the rest of your existence in that dark cave.*

He wails when Loritida stomps his spine and head. And just as the numbness takes over his vital organs, Ryland closes his eyes and exhales his last breath. *And Doramae . . . I will make sure no one ever knows about you. You'll be forgotten forever.*

Doramae roars so loudly that Baronyx stops his flight and flips around to catch sight of the commotion. Jasmyn, Patricia, and Gustavo watch in horror as Doramae and Loritida tear the white dragon's legs, head, and tail from his torso. They shoot streams of fire upon Ryland's carcass, stomping on the blazing pile of flesh, and roar again before jumping into flight.

Moving his enormous wings as fast as he can, stretching his dragon neck forward, Baronyx presses hard to the summit. He glides over the daisy-covered hillsides and swoops up the jagged edges of the oncoming mountain range.

Frosty air blasts the three passengers as Baronyx soars up the atmosphere in a vertical climb. Jasmyn, Patricia, and Gustavo cover their faces against the icy wind and grip Baronyx's fingers with all their might as white blankets of snow flow off the mountains, blown sideways by the storm.

Once Baronyx reaches the top, he slows enough to drop everyone into a thick snowbank just before Doramae and Loritida slam into his body.

Loritida clamps down on Baronyx's back with all four clawed feet, and Doramae clenches her jaws on his front legs and jams her hooks into his torso. Baronyx roars as the three dragons spin wildly in the air, then disappear over the edge of the mountain.

After rolling in the snow for several seconds, Patricia lurches to her feet and searches for Jasmyn. A brusque squall blows snow all around. She pushes through the thigh-high bed of snow and screams, "Jasmyn! Gustavo! Jasmyn!"

When she comes to the edge of the mountaintop, she spots the dragon battle below. She is transfixed as Doramae and Loritida slam Baronyx down onto a pinnacle. With their combined brute force, the peak pierces Baronyx's back like a sharp knife. His ancient roars echo louder than the thunder above, and Patricia covers her ears as the sound scratches at her eardrums.

Baronyx's body flails so abruptly that it thrusts Doramae and Loritida up and away from him, sending them in uncontrollable spins down hundreds of feet. Baronyx separates the pinnacle from the mountain and pulls out the spike stuck in his torso. He roars as blood sprays out from the gash, and he struggles to maintain his flight.

Patricia shouts Jasmyn's and Gustavo's names again, desperately searching for them in the thick field of snow.

"Patricia!" Jasmyn shouts, waving at her. "Up here!"

As Patricia staggers up the small hill, Loritida shoots up behind her, swoops in low, and opens her jaw wide. Jasmyn shields Patricia from Loritida's attack, and the dragon's enormous teeth slam hard onto an invisible shield.

Loritida whines and flings a loose boulder at Jasmyn. Although Jasmyn shields herself, a sliver smashes her shin, shattering her tibia and sweeping her off her feet. Jasmyn rolls onto her back and wails.

Patricia shoots a dozen boulders up at Loritida, knocking her off her flight trajectory and sending her over the edge. When she darts up the hill, Patricia finds blood splattered in the field of white with Jasmyn lying in the middle. She drops to her knees and clears the snow around them.

Gustavo arrives next to her, tugs off his jacket and sweater, and tears the sleeves off his sweater to dress Jasmyn's wound. The sky thunders, and icy hail showers them.

"We have to go to the highest point," Jasmyn says through gritted teeth. She points to the top of the peak, about five hundred feet away.

"Take her," Patricia shouts at Gustavo over the biting rain. She lifts her arm and clears a path in the deep snow. "I'll hold them off."

"You have to come with me!" Jasmyn shouts. "You have to take Uncle Gus's knife and stab me in the heart."

"What?" Patricia and Gustavo shout in unison.

"The time-reversal spell requires a sacrifice, but we can't kill ourselves. Someone has to stick the knife in my heart."

"That's insane!" Gustavo shouts.

"I saw Ryland's vision," Jasmyn replies, looking up at Patricia longingly. "You and Finna were the last survivors of the Foreman Clan attack. You plunged the knife into her heart. You helped Finna execute the spell."

Patricia stares at Jasmyn, agape. She glances at Gustavo, unable to say anything.

"I saw the whole thing," Jasmyn says, drawing her attention. "You stabbed Finna in the heart, and now you have to do the same to me."

Their gazes lock, and Patricia grimaces and shakes her head.

"You have to do this, Patricia."

After another moment, Doramae and Loritida appear in the sky. In a heartbeat, Patricia lifts her arms and thrusts them back. She slams her hands together, and when the dragons collide and fall to the earth, the ground shakes and knocks her off her feet.

Doramae lifts her head and shoots a stream of fire at them.

Patricia rises to her feet just in time to form a wide shield to protect them from the flames.

All at once, the snow vanishes, and Jasmyn gazes out at a red desert stretching for miles. She glances down at her leg—the pain is gone. Her heart races.

What happened?

Then she sees them—her brother and sister standing on the red sand in front of her, their flesh falling off their bones, scowling at her.

"We're dead!" Logan screams and points his bloody finger. "And it's all your fault."

Katarina glares at her, rage gleaming in her eyes. "Don't we mean anything to you? Why did you kill us?" she demands.

Jasmyn yelps, panic pulsing through her. "I didn't kill you." She takes in a shaky breath. "I tried to save you . . . I tried to save both of you but . . ."

"It's all your fault!" Katarina shouts louder. "You let us die! I hate you! We both hate you!"

Jasmyn narrows her eyes. Katarina's anger is out-of-character. Even in her worst nightmares never has her little sister acted this way. She grimaces, closes her eyes, and shakes her head, summoning to mind all she knows to be true.

You're not real. You're both dead. I'm on the mountain. We're fighting Loritida and Doramae. My leg is broken. There's snow all around. And I will execute the time-reversal spell or die trying.

Gustavo shakes her shoulders and shouts her name, but Jasmyn doesn't hear his words. She scrunches her eyelids tighter.

She clenches her teeth, inhales deeply, and shouts, "You're not real! You're! Not! Real!"

When Jasmyn opens her eyes, her siblings are gone. She

breathes heavily against the icy wind, sweat beading on her forehead despite the cold.

"Take her!" Patricia shouts to Gustavo as the stream of fire dies down. "Now!"

Gustavo picks up Jasmyn and runs. Jasmyn screams in agony, her blood forming a trail in the snow.

When he arrives on top of the hill, he puts Jasmyn down, and they watch Patricia battle Loritida while Baronyx struggles with Doramae.

Shivering in the icy rain, Jasmyn shouts through trembling teeth. "You have to do it, Uncle Gus!"

"Do what?"

"Use your knife. It was blessed. It's sacred." She points to her chest. "Right here."

"What? No." Gustavo shakes his head. "I can't. I—"

Jasmyn screams as she sees Loritida looming, about to stomp them.

With her hands in an eagle-claw shape, Patricia spins like a shot-put thrower to propel the winds into a spiral, trapping Loritida in the swirl and sending her slamming into the side of a nearby mountain. The motion jerks Patricia's body into the air, and she tumbles over the ledge. She rolls downhill for a few seconds before hitting an upward scooping ledge that catches her.

When Loritida rolls down the same ridge, Patricia stands up, forms the core rock of a nearby mountain into dozens of enormous spears, and jabs them all into Loritida's torso, stabbing until Loritida's limbs tear into bloody pieces. The dragon releases one last ear-piercing shriek before Patricia severs her head and silences Loritida forever.

After a long sigh, Patricia looks up at the peak that seems miles away. With her wrists sore from the tumble and her knees and elbows bruised, against the hail and wind, she climbs toward the summit. She begs the whirring wind to push her, to help her climb, but she receives no reply.

Fine. Don't help me. Help Jasmyn. She needs you now.

The sun battles through the dark clouds and flashes a ray of light before hiding again, as if to remind Jasmyn of its presence, as if giving her hope. Jasmyn looks up at her uncle with pleading eyes.

"You have to do it, Uncle Gus. Before they come back."

Gustavo shakes his head. "I told your mother I would die for you, sacrifice myself for you. And I promised myself that, if anything happened to you, I'd jump off the nearest bridge. I never promised to"—he swallows hard at the thought—"stick a knife through your heart. What if it doesn't work?"

"It will work."

"You don't know that. You've never done this before. There's a chance it won't work and you'll just . . . die."

Jasmyn nods. "That's true. There's a chance I won't do it right. But, if we don't do this, we will all certainly die. It's a risk we have to take."

After another shaky breath, Gustavo slides his great-grandfather's knife out of the sheath on his belt and looks at his niece.

Except he doesn't see an eighteen-year-old sorceress about to sacrifice her life for her brother and sister. He sees a five-year-old girl who loves to ride on his shoulders and calls him her own personal pony. Her long strands of auburn hair would cover his face as she leaned forward and looked upside down at her strong uncle. Her innocent giggles echo in his ears, and the tiny sound of her voice calling his name fills his mind.

"For Kat. For Logan," Jasmyn shouts. She swallows hard. "For all of us. Please, Uncle Gus. You have to do it."

He nods, and a second later, in the white snow in front of

him, Katarina appears before his eyes, running across a wide field of daisies on a bright sunny day. He gasps, and whispers, "Is that . . . Kat?"

"No Uncle Gus! That's not Kat. That's Doramae. She's putting images in your head! Don't believe it. Kat's dead!"

Gustavo doesn't hear anything but the sweet giggles of his eight-year-old niece as she runs to him. The midday sun bounces off her auburn hair, and her white dress flows playfully in the spring breeze. Gustavo drops the knife, stands up, and walks past Jasmyn with his arms stretched out to the side, ready to receive Katarina's embrace.

"No Uncle Gus! No! She's not real! None of it is real!" Jasmyn cries out, reaching up toward him as he steps away. She turns onto her stomach to drag herself forward, but it's too late—Doramae snatches her uncle up in her claws before Jasmyn can do anything to stop her. The yellow dragon takes Gustavo's legs with one clawed foot and his torso with the other and effortlessly splits his body in two, then tosses him over the mountain's edge.

"No!" Jasmyn shouts with all her soul, with all her heart.

She locks on the yellow dragon and, in a matter of two seconds, all her memories with her uncle, her few sweet moments with her brother and sister, all the happy recollections of her family that she now cherishes fast-forward through her mind, rushing by as if time is running out. She slumps sideways and cries into the ground, unable to see a way to complete the spell, unable to see how she can survive this.

Then, with the loudest scream she has ever produced, Patricia chisels a gigantic skewer of rock from the mountain she stands upon and flings it at the dragon with all her might. The mammoth spear pierces Doramae's body and sends the dragon backward a mile, pinning her to another mountain.

The ground shakes, and Patricia runs to Jasmyn, trying to

194

balance against the earthquake she's created. She picks up Gustavo's knife, flips Jasmyn onto her back, and looks her straight in the eyes.

"Ready?" Patricia shouts as the rock crackles around them.

Matching the determination in Patricia's eyes, Jasmyn shouts, "As is my bloodline's right, I will relive my memories, my past, my history. This is the new truth, and what has been will be no more."

Jasmyn nods, and Patricia slams Gustavo's blessed knife into Jasmyn's chest and straight into her heart. Jasmyn gasps, and the entire mountain collapses around her.

As they descend into the earth alongside broken rock and sheets of ice and snow, Jasmyn imagines Katarina dressed in pink princess pajamas, spinning in her bedroom with her arms spread wide, her messy hair flapping about, singing a silly song. And before ancient earth and stone come crashing down upon Jasmyn, before she hits the bottom of the abyss, everything goes black and her consciousness fades into nothing.

31

RESTART

When Jasmyn opens her eyes, she sees the neon-yellow glow of a model solar system on Katarina's bedroom ceiling, complete with shooting stars and cartoon spaceships. The glow-in-the-dark stickers confuse Jasmyn—it's been years since she's slept in Katarina's room. She closes her eyes, allowing sleep to dominate her. Her questions evaporate with each deep breath.

After a few seconds, just before her body relaxes back into an unconscious state, she remembers her dream.

Dragons, sorceresses, magic . . .

It all seems so fantastical and unbelievable, wilder than any dream she's ever had. As the details of the dream unravel in her mind, with the dragon roars echoing in her ears and the intense heat of fire burning her skin, as she hears her uncle shouting her name, Logan crying out, and Katarina begging for her mother as she dies in Jasmyn's arms, Jasmyn sits up abruptly and gasps.

Then she notices that Katarina is not lying next to her.

She grimaces. "No, no, no, no, no," she whispers, clenching the pink princess comforter. "Where is she?"

Her lip trembles. She stands up and looks around Katarina's room, desperate for a sign of her, for anything to indicate that she is alive, proof that the time-reversal spell worked and that she has come back to a time before her sister's death.

"It had to work," Jasmyn whispers as she searches for clues in Katarina's room.

She whips the comforter off the bed, along with all the

pink and purple pillows. A stuffed lizard flies across the room, bouncing on Katarina's table and knocking coloring books and crayons onto the floor.

"It must have worked. How else could I be here? How else could I still be alive?"

A thought hits her core, and she drops to her knees. Voices in her head repeat the same idea—magic determines its own fate, its own destiny, its own mortality. This is the reason Agatha's magic passed on to both Katarina and Jasmyn, even though Agatha never actually chose a successor. Her magic wanted to live on, in any way it could. It chose to survive.

Jasmyn shakes her head as the idea coalesces in her mind—maybe, instead of turning back the clock, maybe magic saved Jasmyn from the collapsing mountains on the Isle of Enid and transported her to Katarina's bedroom because it was Jasmyn's last thought, the last image in her mind before she lost consciousness.

Magic does what it must to live on.

"No." Jasmyn frowns and shakes her head desperately. "It can't be. The spell must have worked." She grimaces to hold back her cries, denying any dignity to the insane thought that magic chose to only have her survive the whole ordeal.

"No. It can't be," she says in a low voice, almost a growl. She drops to her knees. "Kat has to be alive. Kat has to be here."

"I'm right here!"

When Jasmyn looks up, four-year-old Katarina stands in the doorway in pink princess pajamas too long for her tiny frame. With her mouth agape, Jasmyn sits back on her feet and simply stares at her baby sister. Tears flow down her cheeks.

"What?" Katarina shrugs her small shoulders. "I had to pee."

Logan, now age twelve, far shorter and scrawnier than the

197

last time Jasmyn saw him, appears next to Katarina in the doorway, yawning.

"What happened here?" he asks, scanning the mess in Katarina's room, his eyes wide. "What did you do?"

Without taking another breath, Jasmyn stumbles over to her younger brother and baby sister and hugs them harder than she has ever hugged them in her entire life.

All the mistakes, all the horrible behavior of the past four years, all the death and chaos she's created have been undone.

With every ounce of energy in her body, through the tears spilling from her eyes and the whimpers she can't control, Jasmyn gives thanks to the universe, nature, the gods, and everything around her for this second chance. This time around, she will not take their love for granted. This time around, she will make sure they know that she loves them.

"I think she had a bad dream," Katarina moans, struggling to speak through Jasmyn's tight embrace.

"More like a nightmare," Logan groans as Jasmyn's arm squeezes his neck.

Through the sobs, Jasmyn inhales and says, "It was the worst nightmare ever."

~ ~ ~

It's unlike Jasmyn to be up early on a Saturday morning making breakfast, so when Paula and Kevin walk into the kitchen and smell pancakes, they both freeze and stare at their oldest daughter.

"What's going on?" Paula asks, brows furrowing.

Jasmyn glances back at her parents. "I'm making pancakes."

Paula glances at Katarina and Logan eating at the kitchen

198

table, and she and Kevin both shrug, perplexed.

"We can see that," Kevin says, searching the kitchen for clues. "The question is *why* are you making pancakes?"

"No reason."

In a cool and calm manner, Jasmyn carries the last batch of pancakes to the table. She gives her parents a good-morning kiss on their cheeks and sits down to eat. She wants to apologize for all the suffering they experienced in her other life due to her actions, but she resists the urge and eats her breakfast.

My other life. Jasmyn huffs, stabs a pancake with her fork, and places it on her plate. Silence falls over the kitchen as she drizzles maple syrup onto the pancake.

"Aren't you eating?" she asks her parents after stuffing a bite into her mouth.

Kevin and Paula slowly walk to the kitchen table and kiss Logan and Katarina on their heads before taking their seats. Jasmyn serves a pancake on each of their plates.

"Save some for Nana," Katarina says. "She'll be up soon."

Jasmyn's heart flutters, and she takes a sip of her juice to hide her nerves about seeing her grandmother alive again. She stares at her plate and avoids everyone else's gaze.

"Here," Paula says to Katarina, placing two pills on the napkin in front of her. "Don't forget to take them after you finish eating."

Paula returns to the kitchen counter and stares into space. She is lost in thought, chewing another piece of pancake with little enjoyment, as if she is eating out of obligation.

Jasmyn spots the bags under her eyes, something she's never noticed before.

"Dad, are you taking me to my game?" Logan stuffs a whole pancake into his mouth. "It's an hour away."

"Sorry, Logan, we're taking Kat to her appointment in an

hour."

"I can drive him," Jasmyn says.

Logan laughs and speaks with his mouth full. "Yeah, right, in a couple of years."

Jasmyn holds her breath as she fears her secret is exposed, but when Logan stuffs his face with another pancake and her father chuckles, she breathes. It will take some time getting used to being fourteen again.

"Your uncle said he'd take you. He should be here soon."

When Logan finishes his last pancake and gulps down a tall glass of milk, he sighs with satisfaction and dashes off to his bedroom.

"Wait for me!" Katarina stuffs her pills into her mouth and slurps down a glass of water. She jumps off the chair and skips after Logan.

After a heavy sigh, Paula picks up her plate to take it to the sink.

"I've got it, Mom."

"Thank you, Jaz. Breakfast was delicious. I can't remember the last time I made pancakes."

"Did you see Kat?" Kevin leans back in his chair and stretches, letting out a yawn. "She's full of energy today."

With her hand on Kevin's shoulder, Paula sighs. "Today's a good day."

She kisses his forehead and heads upstairs.

He rubs his eyes and yawns once more, and then reaches for the rest of the plates on the table.

"Leave it, Dad. I'll finish cleaning up."

His weak smile and sad eyes tug at Jasmyn's heart. She's never noticed her parents' exhaustion, the constant concern on their faces, the way they press their lips together to keep from frowning.

Kevin studies her and sighs. "Thank you, Jaz. It's been a long while since we've had a family breakfast. We should do this more often. It's just that your mother and I are so"—he clears his throat—"see . . . Kat's worse than we thought, and—"

"I know, Dad," Jasmyn says. "You don't have to explain. I understand."

"Do you? Because lately you've been . . ." He shifts uncomfortably. "Let's just say I feel like I haven't seen you in weeks. I know we've been busy with Kat's appointments, but even when we're home, you're locked in your room. And when we do see you, you're always mad at us. You have to try and understand, Kat really needs us." He lowers his gaze. "We haven't told you and Logan all the details, but things are very delicate with Kat right now. She needs us, and you have to understand—"

Jasmyn gazes at the tile floor, unable to look her father in the eyes.

It breaks her heart that her father feels the need to explain why he's taking care of his morbidly sick child. She wasn't a stupid kid—Jasmyn should have deciphered what was going on, but her jealousy kept her bitter and angry.

She doesn't interrupt her father's speech. Even though his words pierce her heart, she takes it—she deserves it.

I promise, Dad, you'll never have to give me this speech ever again.

Once he finishes, Jasmyn takes the last set of dishes to the sink, then returns and sits down at the table across from him.

"Dad . . . I've been going through some personal things . . . but I'm fine now. I'm not angry. Not anymore. Trust me. I'm a different person. Things will be different."

He raises his eyebrows. "Really?"

"Yes. Really. I promise. Now, go get ready. I'll finish cleaning up."

201

With a nod, Kevin walks around the table and gives Jasmyn a kiss on her forehead before heading for the stairs.

"Dad?" she calls out.

He looks back at her.

"I'm sorry." She swallows hard. "For everything."

He shakes his head. "There's no need to apologize. It's no one's fault. We're all just trying to get through this."

As he walks out of the kitchen, Jasmyn finally believes, wholeheartedly, for the first time since everything started, that what happened to her family—all the death and destruction that *would* have happened—none of it was her fault.

32

A CHOICE

It has been almost three years since Agatha began experimenting with all sorts of magic to try and cure baby Katarina's ailing health.

The mystical books and artifacts she's collected throughout the centuries from different occults all over the world are well hidden beneath the basement of their local library. While managing the library for most of her mortal life, until she retired, Agatha built the secret room without raising suspicion.

It is where she has spent almost every day for the past three years studying the scriptures, crunching spells, inventing variations in the hopes that she will find a cure. And after every failed session, she returns home with a heavy heart.

Last night was no different.

As usual, she slept deeply, without stirring, as if her mind were too tired to even dream, and she woke up at the crack of dawn to the sound of a dozen birds chirping outside her window. Although she technically rested well, she woke up physically and emotionally exhausted.

She sighs as she plans her day at the library—what books to read, what spells to combine—and she glances out the window, wishing her grandchildren were all vibrant and healthy like those birds with their incessant chirping.

When her grandchildren woke up and ran downstairs earlier, she sat completely still in her chair so they would believe she was still asleep. Every morning, she mentally prepares herself to face them.

By not finding a cure, Agatha is failing her grandchildren, and every day she has trouble looking into their eyes, especially Katarina's. Logan is busy with his sports and activities and Jasmyn is filled with teenage angst she doesn't know how to address, but bright-eyed Katarina is full of hope and happiness, always wearing a smile, unaware of the fate that awaits her.

If all else fails, if Katarina reaches a point where she can no longer live mortally, then Agatha will do what she has sworn to herself she would never do—make Katarina her successor.

The thought of choosing Katarina as her successor to save her life angers her and makes her feel weak and useless. Long ago, Agatha decided to spare her family the burdens of her magic, swearing her granddaughters would never know how lonely and painful immortality can be. Although it pains her to burden Katarina with her magic, she can't just let her granddaughter die.

It is her last resort.

A burst of wind breezes in through the open window, and the white curtain whips up and knocks over a picture frame. Agatha stands to lift the photo and smiles when she sees all three of her grandchildren in the shot. Jasmyn holds baby Katarina in her arms, cooing at her to make her giggle, and Logan smiles wide even though he has two teeth missing.

She picks up another frame and smiles fondly at Jasmyn's fourth grade school photo. Next to that picture is another shot—a new one, from the beginning of Jasmyn's freshman year.

Time sure does fly. You were a newborn just yesterday, and now look at you—a beautiful, intelligent teenager full of potential. I just wish you weren't so angry all the time.

She inhales the fresh spring air and closes her eyes.

So much time is wasted being angry at everything, and the only sure thing to come of it is misery and regret. She sighs once more. *I hope you grow out of it, Jaz, because if I must choose Kat as my successor in order to save her life, she will need her big sister more than ever.*

A creak in the floorboard by her bedroom door breaks her reverie. She opens her eyes and sees Jasmyn holding a tray, peeking past the open door.

"Hi, Nana," Jasmyn says softly, opening the door fully with her foot. "Can I come in? I made breakfast."

"Of course." Agatha inhales the sweet scent of buttermilk pancakes. "Smells delicious."

In the way that Agatha and the women of her bloodline can sense a person's intentions, anxieties, and joys, she senses the dramatic change in Jasmyn's aura. It has been dimming in shades of gray for the past few years, since Katarina was born. But now it shines a strong, solid violet—the color of perseverance, strength, and fortitude, yet also of emotional vulnerability.

In the second it takes to look over her granddaughter from head to toe, Agatha sees that Jasmyn has been through a great ordeal, an odyssey filled with pain and loss. Jasmyn's presence pulls on Agatha's skin. By the fear she sees in her eyes, she can tell that her granddaughter is both eager for and in dread of a conversation about her journey.

Jasmyn stands still in the doorway, as if waiting to be invited in a second time.

Instead of addressing Jasmyn's hesitation, Agatha softens her guard. "Do you remember that pancake dream you had, with the dragons?" She waves her hand for Jasmyn to come in.

After placing the tray on the wide dresser opposite the windows, Jasmyn takes a seat at the foot of her grandmother's bed. "The one where the dragons blew fire on the giant pancakes to char them?"

"Yes, that one." Agatha smiles. "There was an ogre, right?"

"Yes. They were his pancakes. The dragons were trying to steal the pancakes from the ogre."

"You've always had the most amazing dreams." Her eyes wrinkle at the corners.

Jasmyn exhales shakily. "I think your stories produced those images in my head."

"Possibly. Or maybe you're just a storyteller in training." She smiles again and sighs. "You used to tell me the wildest things . . . giant ogres, pink mountains, hairy sharks . . . you have a vivid imagination. You used to tell me every little detail of those dreams."

Agatha stares longingly at Jasmyn. "You used to tell me everything."

An emotional surge rises unexpectedly within Agatha, and she turns away toward the window to hide it. A soft breeze sends the white strands of hair back and away.

After a few breaths, she turns around and faces Jasmyn, her eyes soft and her eyebrows arched with concern. "I know I've been somewhat absent lately, but you know I'm still here for you." She places her hand on Jasmyn's cheek. "You know that, right?"

Jasmyn blinks softly as her grandmother's soft hands caresses her cheek. She inhales deeply, her chest filling up. "I know."

"You can still talk to me."

"I know, Nana."

With the slow grace of woman in her eighties, Agatha walks over to sit next to Jasmyn. "Then why don't you tell me what's on your mind, the way you used to when you were little?"

"Nana . . ." Jasmyn looks at her hands folded on her lap.

"I'm listening."

And in a quick breath, as if trying to explain everything in ten seconds, Jasmyn says, "I know about your magic, about your mother Finna, about Patricia and Regina and all about the Foreman Clan and . . ." Jasmyn swallows hard, rubs her hands together, and whispers, "I know everything."

Agatha's heart pounds so loudly it's the only thing she can hear. Mouth agape, she stares at Jasmyn, dumbfounded. Her stomach is in knots, and she feels lightheaded.

"Nana? Did you hear me?" Jasmyn leans in closer. "I know about your magic. I know about everything."

After a few silent seconds, as a tear rolls down Agatha's wrinkled cheek, she finally finds her voice. "How do you know?" She swallows through the dryness in her throat.

Jasmyn's bottom lip trembles for several seconds before she proceeds to tell Agatha the whole story, leaving nothing out. Agatha asks questions when something seems unclear, and Jasmyn answers with what she knows to be true. She even shares her sense of guilt, of which Agatha absolves her and claims full ownership.

After three hours of what seems like an incredible tale, interrupted by moments of intense sobs and consolation, Jasmyn and Agatha both sigh the most satisfying sigh of relief.

"I can't believe Patricia was there with you at the end. It's an incredible coincidence."

"She never gave up on me." Jasmyn smiles softly.

A knot materializes in Agatha's throat, and her voice cracks. "I wish I hadn't given up on her."

"There's still time. You can always reach out to her."

"Oh no." She places her hand on Jasmyn's. "I'll leave it to you to connect with her. Magic is a young woman's game."

Agatha stands and reaches for a jewelry box on her dresser. She opens it and moves around a few items before pulling out the dragon amulet. She sits back down next to Jasmyn. "When I told you the story of why this relic was created," Agatha says, lifting up her fingers in a pinch, "I was *this* close to telling you everything. But you were so excited about the magical fantasy that I just couldn't spoil it for you. You were so young."

Jasmyn studies her grandmother as she gazes upon the relic, shaking her head, smiling tenderly.

"You know, of all my treasures and heirlooms, this is probably my most valuable." Agatha offers the amulet to Jasmyn. "I want you to have it."

Jasmyn shakes her head. "I can't. I don't deserve it."

"Yes, you do. I promised it to you long ago. And if I learned anything from your amazing journey, there's no time like the present." Agatha hangs the charm around Jasmyn's neck and gazes softly at her.

"So . . . what now?" Jasmyn asks with eager eyes.

"Well, since taking my magic to the grave won't work, I will have to choose between you and Kat to inherit my magic. I don't want history to repeat itself." She stares into her granddaughter's eyes. "Who do you think I should choose?"

"I don't know."

"Okay. Let me put it another way . . . do you think you should inherit my magic?"

Jasmyn looks down and doesn't answer.

"Should I give it to Kat?"

"No!" Jasmyn lurches up. She takes a deep breath and sits back down, avoiding her grandmother's gaze.

Agatha winces at Jasmyn's quick response. "Oh? Why not?"

"She's so young—she's only a kid. She doesn't even know what death really means. I mean . . . she's all about princesses and pink and purple dresses and . . . even if you wait until you pass away, she will only be eight. She is still so innocent. There's so much history, and death, and loss in your life, and . . .

208

it's a lot for Kat."

"So, you think I should choose you."

"No. I don't want it." Jasmyn glances to the side. "But . . . I don't want Kat to . . ." Her voice cracks, and she swallows back the knot in her throat.

Agatha tilts her head and waits a few seconds. "You don't want Kat to what?"

Jasmyn stands up again and reaches for a photo of a laughing baby Katarina. The frame is bordered by a line of white daisies, and Jasmyn traces the outline of the petals with her fingers. She stares at Katarina's wide baby grin, a moment perfectly frozen in time.

"I don't want her to lose that bright look in her eyes," Jasmyn says softly.

She places the frame back on the dresser and faces Agatha. "If she gets all your memories, the death, the pain and loss, the suffering . . . she might lose that look in her eyes that's always full of hope and optimism. And I will live my entire life knowing I chose to burden her." She shakes her head. "I can't let her carry it, knowing what it is. It's not fair to her. First her heart, and now this? It's not fair to make her suffer more." She stands up and paces around Agatha's bed. "It's not fair."

As Jasmyn purses her lips, internally arguing with herself, Agatha smirks and recalls feeling the same frustration when she met Elliot on the beach that fateful spring day. She spent the rest of the night cursing the universe for introducing Elliot into her life when she finally had a path to the Isle of Enid to undo all her misery and suffering.

But when Elliot appeared on her doorstep the following morning for their breakfast date, shining that mesmerizing smile, Agatha's mind was made up.

"It has to be me," Jasmyn says with a frown. She sits back

down on the bed, bends over, and grimaces, covering her face. "I don't want it, but I can't make Kat suffer through it." She wipes her cheeks and regains her composure.

After a few seconds, with the calmness of an adult who has traveled to the ends of the world and back, Jasmyn sits tall, and says, "It has to be me."

"Are you sure?" Agatha shifts to face Jasmyn directly. "This can't be undone."

She nods with certainty and releases a loud breath. "It can only be me. Can we do it now, so I don't have to think about it anymore? I just want to make sure what happened in my last lifetime never happens again."

Agatha nods back, takes her successor's hands into her own and gazes upon her with fondness. She has never been so proud of her granddaughter.

"This won't hurt a bit."

33

A NEW BEGINNING

Despite many attempts at addressing the cancerous tumor that spread to her brain, Agatha could not alter her own condition. Aggressive cancer is a formidable mortal foe, and no known magic can stop it—especially when you've asked for it.

When Agatha discovered a spell that would save Katarina at the price of dying a slow, cancer-filled, dementia-riddled, painful death, she wasted no time.

Soon after Katarina's miraculous recovery, cancer was discovered all over Agatha's body. It was a small price to pay for this centuries-old sorceress, a sacrifice she would have made for any one of her grandchildren.

And even though Jasmyn knew when her grandmother was going to die, her death was hard to bear. She never shared the exact date with anyone, not even Agatha, as her grandmother had requested. It was the least Jasmyn could do for her grandmother.

The funeral parlor is still full of guests toward the end of Agatha's wake.

Jasmyn stands at the front of the room next to a display of photos showcasing her grandmother's life. As she shakes the hand of the pastor and thanks him for the sermon, an unfamiliar shock travels through her body—the electric, hair-raising, heart-pounding sensation a sorceress feels when another sorceress is close by.

She scans the room and spots Patricia in the doorway.

In her memories from years ago, memories that never

happened in this lifetime, perhaps enhanced in the way everyone enhances unforgettable memories, Jasmyn remembers Patricia as a woman of exceptional strength and fortitude, yet loving and supportive. Comforting embraces and words of encouragement echo in her mind as she recalls their time together, special moments that Patricia herself will never experience.

Although Patricia has always claimed she was in a dark place when Agatha died, it's hard for Jasmyn to imagine it. Jasmyn has placed her coven sister so high on a pedestal that when Patricia narrows her eyes at her and scowls, her stomach sinks.

Agatha advised Jasmyn against contacting Patricia or Regina until after her passing, to allow events to unfold naturally. She also cautioned Jasmyn against looking for Caderyn or Ryland, to thwart any retribution Ryland might cook up after he finds out about Jasmyn's use of the time-reversal spell.

"He will eventually find out," Agatha had said, "but it might take decades, centuries even. By then, I'll be gone, and you will have had time to get to know Patricia and Regina. Don't do anything now. You have time."

Unfortunately for Agatha, Jasmyn didn't inherit her grandmother's patience.

In her junior year, Jasmyn convinced her mother to take her to England to visit Oxford and Cambridge. Her academic performance meant she might get accepted to either school, so Paula made it happen.

On the trip, Jasmyn broke into Ryland's underground chambers and stole the dragon eggs undetected. She carefully packed the eggs in damage-proof packaging and used her magic to keep them hidden from Paula, airport security, and the flight attendants.

When she showed Agatha her souvenir from England, Agatha gasped. "Ryland and the Foreman Clan will come looking for you," she said, worry in her eyes.

"Don't worry, Nana," Jasmyn said with a satisfied smile. "Like you said, I have time before Ryland learns the truth. By then, Patricia and Regina and I will be ready. And if Ryland comes sooner, well . . . I know Baronyx and his brother dragons will help me deal with the Foreman Clan." She took Agatha's hand. "I promise, everything will be fine."

Agatha accepted the explanation with a sigh of relief.

But what Agatha didn't know, what Jasmyn decided not to tell her, was that she'd left Ryland a note in the crate that had held the dragon eggs.

The note read, "The dragons are no longer yours. Along with the other dragons I possess, you and Caderyn and the Foreman Clan stand no chance. I am not looking for power, only peace. Consider me *not* killing you in your sleep as proof of my intentions. However, if I find out you or Caderyn are looking for me—and trust me, I will know—the next time we meet, I will not be so generous."

Jasmyn remains pleased with her decision to act even though she's likely sped up Ryland's discovery of her existence. With her grandmother's training, with Patricia and Regina at her side, as well as Baronyx and his brother dragons and five more unborn dragons, she knows the odds of defeating Ryland and the Foreman Clan are in her favor.

Now, as Patricia approaches her grandmother's coffin, Jasmyn holds her breath.

"Do you know who I am?" Patricia asks without a hint of emotion on her face.

"I do," Jasmyn says, holding back the urge to hug her. "You're Patricia Winston. You're a powerful sorceress, just like Nana was. You have incredible strength and a considerable temper, and you like to live on your own terms. I have all of Nana's

213

memories, so I know you very well."

"Good." Patricia skims Jasmyn once over. "Did Agatha leave any last words for me?"

"Yes. She said to tell you that she has always loved and respected you, that you always made her proud. She leaves this world with no anger or bitterness, with no grudges, and love for everyone who came into her life."

After a deep breath, Patricia faces the coffin. "Damn, Agatha, you were always good with the sentimental stuff." She faces Jasmyn. "I'm not so good with it."

"I know." Jasmyn smirks.

Patricia nods, and the corner of her lip curves upward. "Seems like Agatha prepared you well."

"She did."

"Jaz?" Gustavo walks toward Jasmyn and catches Patricia's gaze. He's caught off guard by Patricia's beauty and stares at her with his mouth slightly open.

"Uncle Gus?" Jasmyn presses her lips together to suppress a snort.

"Oh." He closes his eyes and shakes his head. "Your parents are leaving to prepare for the reception at the house. Make sure everyone gets the address." He extends his arm toward Patricia for a handshake. "I'm sorry—we haven't met. I'm Gustavo, Jasmyn's uncle."

"This is Patricia Winston, Agatha's friend . . . friend's . . . daughter," Jasmyn says, looking at Patricia with a knowing gaze.

Patricia shakes Gustavo's hand firmly. "Sadly, my mother couldn't make it. She passed away a few weeks ago."

"I'm sorry to hear that." Gustavo steps past Jasmyn and leans in close to Patricia. "You should come to the house."

"Oh, I can't impose."

"It's no imposition. It was Agatha's wish to gather her

friends and family together. She would have loved for you to come. You can't deny a dead woman her last wish. It's bad karma. You'll be cursed with guilt if you don't."

Patricia relents with a half-smile. "Okay. What's the address?"

Jasmyn slips away to greet another guest and tell them about the reception her parents have prepared. It was one of many final wishes Agatha requested along with finding a way to get Patricia and Gustavo to meet. As Jasmyn watches Patricia and Gustavo flirt in the corner of the parlor, it seems she no longer needs to worry about fulfilling that wish.

She gazes over at Agatha's coffin and wonders if she still has some sort of magical influence, even in death.

An hour later, after the last few guests leave, Gustavo takes the photo display down to carry it back to the house. "Jaz, I'm taking these to the car. Can you tell the director we're done?"

"Sure."

"I'll wait in the car."

Once Jasmyn picks up the remaining memorial cards, program pamphlets, and the guest book and stuffs it all into her tote bag, she takes one last moment with Agatha, letting out a long sigh.

This is the last time she'll gaze upon her grandmother, lying in her coffin as if asleep, wearing the white gown she picked. Jasmyn blinks, and sharp images of Katarina and Logan lying dead on the concrete inexplicably flash before her eyes.

These events didn't happen in this lifetime, but they still haunt her nightmares, and sometimes her daydreams. Although it pains her to know her brother and sister died so gruesomely in her last life, she is strangely thankful that the images appear from time to time. They are a reminder of what occurred, of what can happen if she lets things get out of hand. It's part of her penance, and she accepts it stoically.

She takes one long, last look at her grandmother. She imagines Nana strolling on the shores of the Isle of Enid, wearing the same white dress she's wearing now, her white hair flowing in the breeze. She pictures dragons flying in the clear blue sky and women congregating on the shore.

Jasmyn kisses the tips of her fingers and taps Agatha's forehead. "Thank you, Nana, for everything."

~ ~ ~

As Gustavo drives home, Jasmyn peruses the entries in the guest book. "Hey! Mrs. Gloria Santiago, Brian's mom . . . she was at the funeral!" she says excitedly. "I didn't see her."

"She came with Brian and her mother, Ines. They left early because they had to catch a flight to Chile. Big family reunion."

Jasmyn gasps, pulse pounding. "Brian was there too?"

"Yeah. He helped me set up the photo display. He's huge! He was tiny when I last saw him."

"I can't believe I missed him . . . I mean, them."

"Gloria said Ines was a member of Agatha's senior center. Just a few months ago, they started writing to each other, real letters in the mail. In fact, they left a card. It was thick."

"Where is it?"

"I gave it to your mom."

Jasmyn's heart flutters. It has been almost a year since she stopped thinking of Brian Santiago. Although she promised Brian that she would look for him when she went back, she's never worked up the courage.

How can she tell him what really happened? Time travel? Dragons? Sorcery? He would never believe her. And if she finds him and chooses not to tell him the truth, then she has to live her entire life with this incredible lie.

What if they do meet and it doesn't work out because there's no chaos to bring them together, no drama to open the floodgates of intense emotion?

What if they're too different, totally incompatible, and the dream that was a once-in-a-lifetime romance fizzles into nothing but a bad date?

No matter how many times Agatha encouraged Jasmyn to contact him, Jasmyn rationally convinced herself otherwise. She promised herself she wouldn't go looking for him, she wouldn't try and force a romance that never existed.

She's stuck to her promise all these years. The last thing on her mind was the possibility of her grandmother scheming to get them together. She wonders what she wrote to Brian's grandmother. Jasmyn shakes her head and smiles.

At the end of the evening, after everyone's left the house, as Jasmyn wipes down the kitchen counter, she comes upon the plastic bag of sympathy cards Paula and Kevin collected from the guests. She drops her rag, sits down at the counter, and opens each card, reading them one by one.

After several cards and letters, Jasmyn comes across a thick yellow envelope. She tears the top, pulls out the contents, and flips the card open. A smaller blue envelope drops onto her lap.

For Jasmyn, it reads.

She gasps. "No way."

After staring in awe at the sealed blue envelope, she opens it and pulls out a folded letter. She takes a deep breath and reads.

Dear Jasmyn,

I am so sorry for your loss. I know it's been a while since we've spoken, but I want you to know that I'm here if you need someone to talk to, someone who understands what goes on inside the crazy mind of a football-helmet-wearing space marine. There aren't many of us left in this world. We have to stick together.

Yours truly,
Brian

And there it is—proof that there are things in the universe meant to be a certain way, designed to follow a certain path, that can never be changed even by the most life-altering events.

So much is different in this lifetime, but some things, like her uncle's dedication to his family, Patricia's loyalty to her coven, secrets to be kept, enemies to watch for, and, evidently, the love of a young boy for a little girl pretending to be a space marine . . . some truths are so powerful, so permanent, so transcending, that they are entirely untouchable by magic.

~ THE END ~

ACKNOWLEDGEMENTS

I want to thank my brother, Norberto, for giving me the confidence I needed to continue with the series. He was an avid reader of fantasy and science fiction. Shelves of books lined his bedroom. We were at our town pool when I handed him a print review copy of the first book in the *Family Relics* series, *The Box of Souls*. He sat down on a pool lounge chair and read ¾ of the book in one sitting. He also got a bad sunburn that day. And when book two, *The Onyx Ring*, was released, he read it in a couple of days, then asked when the last book would come out. Sadly, he passed away suddenly just a few months later.

Although it took two years for me to restart the manuscript for the last book in the series, I felt my brother's presence guide me through this last book. He was in the military for over twenty years, and I witnessed personally how his military brothers and sisters regarded one another. It truly is a family of its own. His real-life example led me to create Jasmyn's uncle Gustavo and the characters that surround him. His sense of service, his family loyalty, his undeniable love for his niece and nephew. For that, I am forever grateful. I hope I did him justice.

I want to thank Catherine Jones Payne of Quill Pen Editorial for being patient with me and my wishy-washy timing. The first draft was missing something, and I could not find it. It was missing a lot of things, but with Catherine's developmental editing, she helped me discover what was buried underneath it all and helped me bring it out into the story it is today. I could never have reached this point without her.

And Jenny Zemanek, my cover designer, who also allowed me to delay and reschedule, because life was just crazy for all of us. The first two covers were amazing, and when there was a slight possibility that I might not have her for the 3rd cover, I nearly cried. Thankfully, it all worked out and the cover is fantastic.

To my husband who roots me on in almost everything I do, and to my daughter and son for talking me up as a "real author" to their friends, you are my treasures.

And finally, to everyone who chose to purchase my books, thank you a million times over. I hope you enjoyed reading them as much as I enjoyed writing them.

ABOUT THE AUTHOR

Tanya Miranda grew up daydreaming about everything. From human-looking aliens hiding in the government, to witches and dragons skulking in the shadowy corners of her basement, to finding the love of her life running through a hailstorm, her imagination never ceases to create kooky characters in the most bizarre circumstances. Her one true wish is to draw the images that materialize in her head. Until then, she'll continue to put her dreams into stories.

To find out more about this author's writing, visit her at:
www.tanyamiranda.com